Book Fourteen

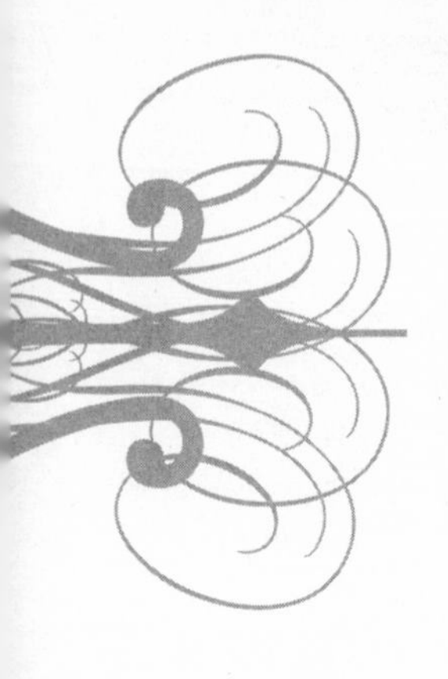

Sweep

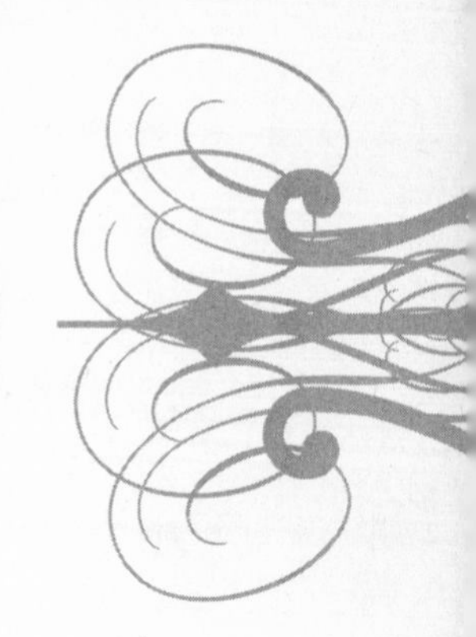

Cate Tiernan

FULL CIRCLE

speak
An Imprint of Penguin Group (USA) Inc.

To those who struggled to keep Sweep alive

All quoted materials in this work were created by the author.
Any resemblance to existing works is accidental.

Full Circle

Published by the Penguin Group
Penguin Group (USA) Inc., 345 Hudson Street, New York, New York 10014, U.S.A.
Penguin Group (Canada), 90 Eglinton Avenue East, Suite 700, Toronto, Ontario M4P 2Y3, Canada
(a division of Pearson Penguin Canada Inc.)
Penguin Books Ltd, 80 Strand, London WC2R 0RL, England
Penguin Group (Australia), 250 Camberwell Road, Camberwell, Victoria 3124, Australia
(a division of Pearson Australia Group Pty Ltd)
Penguin Group (NZ), 67 Apollo Drive, Rosedale, North Shore 0632, New Zealand
(a division of Pearson New Zealand Ltd)
Penguin Books (South Africa) (Pty) Ltd, 24 Sturdee Avenue,
Rosebank, Johannesburg 2196, South Africa

Published by Puffin Books, a division of Penguin Young Readers Group, 2002
This edition published by Speak, an imprint of Penguin Group (USA) Inc., 2009

5 7 9 10 8 6

Cover Photography copyright 2001 Barry David Marcus
Photo-illustration by Marci Senders
Series Design by Russell Gordon

Produced by 17th Street Productions,
an Alloy company
151 West 26th Street
New York, NY 10001

ISBN 978-0-14-241029-5

Printed in the United States of America

www.penguin.com

1

Morgan

Goddess, how did I get here?

I'm barefoot on a narrow, rocky shore, and the sharp pebbles are biting into the bottoms of my feet. I stumble left and right, struggling to walk. The wind picks up, blowing hard, tangling my hair around my face so that it's almost impossible to see. The air smells faintly of brackish water, algae, and fish.

Where am I? How did I get here?

I realize that I'm afraid. I'm incredibly afraid of being here. Every cell in my body is begging to leave this beach. I could take off into the lake or head into the woods that border the water. Anything to get off this rocky shore, where I feel so vulnerable, so alone. Where am I? What lake is this? It's completely unfamiliar. I glance over at the woods, and then a dark shadow appears over me.

Cold. Black. And getting bigger.

My whole body goes rigid. Everything in me knows that this shadow means danger. Looking up, I'm shocked at how close it is, and I reflexively crouch down on the stony shore. Now I can see its source: a huge, dark-feathered hawk, flying just overhead, its vicious, golden eyes glowering. Who are you? my mind screams. What do you want with me? But the hawk has caught sight of something else.

As I watch, consumed with panic, the raptor tucks its wings to its sides and shoots down like an arrow. Ten feet above the water it swings powerful legs forward and slashes at the choppy surface with curved razor claws. A moment later it spreads its wide, dark wings and beats the air, bringing itself upward slowly at first and then with increasing speed. In its talons a large, speckled rainbow trout is twisting frantically, arching back like a bow in an attempt to drop free. As the hawk surges upward, soon to become a small spot against the sky, I see the fish's eyes go blank with death.

The fear I feel is overwhelming, even though the hawk is gone. My whole body feels shaky, numb, as though I had just avoided death myself. Without understanding it, I know the hawk was after me. Is *after me.*

I have to get off this beach!

I run for the trees, the pebbles flaying my feet. Soon I'm limping, stumbling, looking back over my shoulder, desperate to make the line of trees before the hawk returns. Then, just as quickly as the hawk appeared, I'm at the entrance to the woods, and I plunge into darkness. It's cooler. It takes a minute for my eyes to adjust to the shaded light. The ground is covered with pine needles, ground-hugging vines, weathered bits of leaves, all dry and crackly. I look around but can't see any kind of path, any destination. There's a fallen log nearby, and on it is a cluster of pale, spindly mushrooms sprouting up like a tiny Dr. Seuss forest. Large black ants swarm over the log, moving fast in a wavering line.

Oh, Goddess, where am I? Without knowing that, I feel so alone and scared. What woods are these? One thing is clear: I have to find my way out. I'll have to make my own path. A quick glance finds a slightly less overgrown section, and I head for it. I hold slim branches aside as I pass through, heading deeper into the woods.

Then I stand quiet and unmoving in the woods and realize that all of my senses are prickling. Magick. There is magick here. More than the constant low hum of energy that most blood witches pick up on and then ignore as background noise. This is magick being worked, being created, brought into being by design and effort and thought. My skin is tingling, my breathing faster.

Closing my eyes, I cast out my senses, searching for the magick's source. I concentrate, slow my heartbeat, remain perfectly still . . . there. My eyes pop open and automatically search ahead of me at eleven o'clock, north and slightly west. I ease my way through closely grown trees, step over fallen logs and thigh-high vines blocking the way. I get ever closer to that elusive, irresistible vibration, the vibration of a blood witch pulling power out of air. Now the woods' smell of humus, dry bark, fungus, and insects is overlain with crisscrossing ribbons of smoke from burning herbs. Somehow I know, without a doubt, that a powerful blood witch is working this magick, and that she is a stranger to me, and that I could learn from her. My fingers begin to itch with anticipation—what can she teach me? What can I show her of my own powers? My chest fills with both pride and uncertainty: I know I am strong, unusually strong, and have impressed witches much more educated than I. I also know that my successes are sometimes flukes—that my abilities are unpredictable because I am untrained, uninitiated.

I can feel it now, magick threading through the trees like a scent. These vibrations are strange to me—is this good magick being worked? What if it's not? But surely I would pick up on it if it's dark magick. For a moment I hesitate. What if . . . But I press on. Just ahead of me the greenish light filtering through the trees' crowns grows brighter: there's a clearing ahead. I swallow and try to press forward, crashing clumsily through the trees and bushes, slapping the vines aside. This is it—soon, soon I will see the magick worker. Soon I will compare myself to her—she will be more trained and more knowledgeable, but I will be stronger. My throat is tight with excitement. Soon, soon, just another step . . . and then my foot catches on a tree root, throwing me off balance.

As I feel myself falling, my muscles tense and I fling out my arms. My wrist hits something hard with a startling smack. Wild-eyed, I jerk to a sitting position, not able to make sense of what I am seeing. Did I faint? Did the witch put some kind of spell on me?

No. I was in my bedroom, at home. It was quite dark—not yet dawn, it seemed. My bed felt soft and weirdly smooth beneath me since I was expecting the crunchy edges of leaves and twigs. Blinking, I looked around. It had been a dream.

My heart was still racing. In the strange half-light of my bedroom I could still see the hawk above me, still see the glint of its razor-sharp claws as it grabbed the fish. I pushed my damp hair off my face and reassured myself that none of that was real, that everything in my room was just as I had left it the night before. Of course it was. It had just been a dream, that's all. An incredibly realistic, visceral, strong dream.

Slowly I lay back down and flipped my pillow over to the cooler side. I lay blinking up at my ceiling, then glanced at my clock. 5:27. I never wake up that early. It was Saturday. No school. I could go back to sleep for hours if I wanted to. I tried to calm down, but I still felt anxious and headachy. I closed my eyes and deliberately relaxed, willing myself to release all tension and enter into a light meditation. Very quietly I whispered, "Everything is fine and bright. Day must follow every night. My power keeps me safe from harm. The Goddess holds me in her arms."

It was a simple soothing spell, something to help me banish the leftover weirdness from my dream. It hadn't been a *nightmare,* exactly—not all of it. But strange, with some frightening parts that I could hardly remember anymore.

When I opened my eyes again, I felt better, calmer. All the same, I wasn't able to fall back asleep. Instead, I lay on my bed and watched as my room slowly filled with the ever-brightening pink glow of dawn. By six it was definitely light out, and I heard birds chattering and the sounds of the occasional car going by our house. Though my eyes drifted shut, I didn't sleep until I heard my parents get up around seven-thirty. The sounds of them going downstairs, talking softly, the rush of water as Mom filled the coffeemaker—it was the lullaby that finally eased me back to sleep. I had no more dreams and didn't reawaken for another two hours. I heard my younger sister, Mary K., turning on the shower in the bathroom we shared, and I smiled as she started singing a song that had been all over the radio lately.

Everything is fine, I told myself, stretching and yawning loudly. My family was all around me. I was safe in my bed. Later on I would see Hunter, and as usual, just the thought of my boyfriend—his short, white-blond hair, his fathomless green eyes, his intensely attractive English accent—made me shiver pleasantly. Everything was calm and normal, an incredibly nice change when I considered what the past several weeks had been like.

Everything was okay. I was Morgan Rowlands, a blood witch of the Woodbane clan. Tonight I would meet with my coven for our regular Saturday night circle. But now I was going to go downstairs and see if we had any Pop-Tarts.

2

Hunter

"Right," I said. "But why you would use the *second* form of limitations here? This spell is all about place, about where you are, where you want the spell to ignite."

My da nodded. "Aye. But what's its purpose?"

"To make a barrier that would stop something or slow it down," I replied. It was Saturday morning, and Da and I each had about an hour before we had to leave: me for my part-time job at Practical Magick, one of the few very good occult bookstores nearby, and Da for a lecture in a town two hours away. Ever since he had crafted the spell that dismantled a dark wave, he'd been in high demand as a speaker at coven meetings. Witches everywhere were eager to know how to dispel this massive threat, and Da seemed happy to teach them.

Right now, he was teaching me.

"You're right there," said Da. "But is the place in which you set the spell its most important aspect?"

"Of *course*," I said. "If you set this barrier in the wrong place, it's useless."

Da gave me his even look, the one that made me feel like I was particularly slow-witted. He was an incredibly gifted spellcrafter, and I was lucky to have the chance to learn from him. As a Seeker, I had been well trained in many areas but had gotten only the most basic training in spellcraft.

What was he was getting at? I waited, telling myself to stay calm, not to get my hackles up. It wasn't easy: Da and I had had a lot to argue about in the past few months.

"What level of a starr is this?" Da asked, flipping through his Book of Shadows, hardly paying attention.

"What level? This is a . . . a . . ." Oh, *bloody hell!* my brain screamed, recognizing too late the trap I had fallen into. Damn! I *hate* it when I do something stupid. Especially, most especially, in front of my father. I tried to keep burning embarrassment from reddening my face. I had two conflicting feelings: humiliation, over making a mistake in front of my father, and annoyance, about the lecture I knew I was about to receive.

But to my surprise he said, "It's not easy, lad. You could study spellcraft for years and still make mistakes like that. And who knows? There could conceivably be a situation where the exact location of a starr *is* more important than its strength."

I nodded, surprised at this unprecedented display of mercy. "Mum was a great spellcrafter, wasn't she?" I asked the question gently, still feeling the pain myself and knowing how heavily my mother's death, only four months before, had affected my father.

Da's eyes instantly narrowed, as if he had suddenly stepped into sunlight. I saw his jaw muscles tighten, then relax. "Yes," he said, sounding older than he had a moment ago. "She was that." A wistful half smile crossed his face for a moment. "Watching your mother craft spells was like watching a master wood-carver cut complicated figures out of a simple block of wood. It was an amazing thing. My parents and teachers taught me the Woodbane basics when I was a lad, but it was your mother, with her thousand-year Wyndenkell heritage, who taught me the beauty of pure spellcraft."

"I would like to become a master spellcrafter someday," I said. "Like Mum."

Da gave me one of his rare smiles, and it transformed his thin, ravaged face into that of the father I had known so long ago. "That would be a worthy gift, son," he said. "But you have a lot of work ahead of you."

"I know," I said, sighing. I glanced over at the clock and saw that I had about half an hour till I had to leave. It would be midafternoon in England. I had a phone call to make. "Ah, I think I'll ring Kennet now, while I have the chance," I said offhandedly.

The truth was, I was dreading this phone call. A few weeks ago, following our battle with the dark wave, I had decided that I was quitting my position as a Seeker for the International Council of Witches. At seventeen I had become the youngest Seeker in history, and for a time I'd had complete faith in the ICOW's judgment. I had taken great pride in my work, in making the world a safer place for good witches. But that was before the council had failed me in several key areas: neglecting to tell me that they'd found my parents, for one, a decision that resulted in my mum dying before I had the chance to see her and say good-bye. Also, they had failed to warn Morgan and me that her father, Ciaran MacEwan, the leader of a dark coven called Amyranth, had escaped from captivity and might be coming to Widow's Vale to harm us (or to send the dark wave after us, as turned out to be the case).

Da was quiet for a moment. I knew he had his reservations about my quitting the council, but I also knew that I couldn't continue serving a system I no longer trusted. Kennet Muir had once been my mentor and my friend, but he wasn't any longer as far as I was concerned. "Are you quite sure?" Da asked.

"Yes."

"It's not too late to change your mind, you know," he said. "Working at Practical Magick is fine for now, but in the long run, you'll be hurting for a career with more fulfillment. Even if you no longer want to be a Seeker, surely you could find something to challenge you a bit more. I just hope you've thought this through."

"I know, Da. And I have. I just need some time to figure out what the right new career is." Nobody was more frustrated by my lack of direction than I, but you can't spend years dedicated to being a good Seeker and then find something just as fulfilling overnight.

"Perhaps I could help you," Da said, organizing the books we had been using for reference into a clean stack. "I do speak to a wide variety of witches in my spellcrafting lectures. Perhaps one of them . . ."

"No, Da." I shook my head and tried to give him a reassuring smile. "I'll be fine. I just need some time."

He looked like he wanted to say more, but then he nodded and headed to the kitchen. I heard the tap turn on and the sound of water filling the kettle. I fetched Kennet's number and dialed it quickly, before I lost my nerve, even though

I knew it was going to cost a fortune, calling England in the middle of the day. After five rings Kennet's voice-mail system picked up. I grimaced and left a brief message, giving him my mobile number and the number at Practical Magick.

Soon Da headed off to his lecture, not sure if he would be back that night, and I set off for Practical Magick. It was in Red Kill, about twenty minutes north of Widow's Vale, the town in midstate New York where I lived. As I drove, I thought about what Da had said. It was funny. For the last eleven years of my life I'd had no father. Now, at the age of nineteen, I had to get used to having a da to take an interest in me. But he was right about one thing: I did need a new life plan. All around me everyone had a purpose, goals—except me.

The doorbell jingled lightly when I entered Practical Magick. Its owner, Alyce Fernbrake, smiled a greeting at me as she rang up a purchase for a customer. I smiled and waved, then headed through a new doorway that had been cut into the right-hand wall of the store. The room next door was divided in two: a larger room that would stock store items and books, and a smaller room in back that people would be able to use privately. It was in this room that I worked, imbuing objects with low-level magickal properties.

For example, I might spell a small bottle of evening primrose oil so that it would be even more effective in easing menstrual cramps. Or I might spell different candles to increase their individual auras, make them more effective in rites or meditation. Alyce kept a small supply of spelled objects in a locked cupboard in the back room, to be bought and used only by witches she trusted. They didn't have to be blood witches, but she had to know them and be sure these things would be used only in the way they were intended.

For the first couple of days this had been amusing, even relaxing work. It allowed me to trot out all my basic second-year spells, brush up on my technique, my focus, and in general stay in tune with magickal energy. But now I was growing bored and restless. I still enjoyed being at Practical Magick, working with Alyce, but the repetition, the predictability of this job was starting to make me impatient. Da was right—I needed to find a vocation that would challenge me.

I was putting a light worry-not spell on a pale blue candle when my mobile rang, making me jump. I yanked it out of my pocket, then checked the number. It was Kennet, calling me back. I took a deep breath and answered it.

"Kennet. Thanks for calling me back."

"Hunter, how are you? No problems there, I hope?"

Not in the last week, I thought. It seemed that ever since I'd come to Widow's Vale, my life had been a roller coaster of huge events—not the least of which was meeting Morgan Rowlands, who's—well, she's more than my girlfriend. She's my *mùirn beatha dàn*—my soul mate.

I decided to dive right in. "Kennet—you've had trust in me and put enormous effort into my training, and I've always appreciated it. I hope I've never let you down." *Like you've let me down,* I added silently.

"Why do I feel you're about to?" he asked.

I took another breath. "I've decided to leave the council," I said. "I can't be a Seeker anymore."

There was silence on his end. I waited.

"I know you've been growing more and more dissatisfied, Gìomanach," he said, using my coven name. "And I know you were very upset at how the council handled telling you about your parents."

To put it mildly. Just thinking about it made my body tense. "Certainly that's part of it," I said, feeling anger rise up in my chest. "But there have been other problems, Kennet, other disappointments." I let my words hang there in the air for a moment. "The truth is, I feel I can't continue with the council in good faith. Not when I don't believe in it."

More silence. "Gìomanach, you know it's almost unheard of for *anyone* to quit the council, especially a Seeker." His voice was soft, but I sensed some anger behind his words.

"I know," I said. "But I have no choice. So I'm telling you officially—I'm leaving. I can't accept any more assignments. I'm sorry."

"How about a leave of absence?" Kennet asked carefully. "I could certainly okay that."

"No."

"Gìomanach," Kennet said with more authority, "this seems an extreme reaction. Surely it doesn't have to be all or nothing. Would you prefer a different assignment? Or to go to a different place? Perhaps your compensation—"

"No," I said. "It really isn't about any of that. It's just—the council itself."

"Would you like me to come there, to talk to you? Perhaps the two of us could come up with a more moderate decision."

"You can come if you'd like, but I don't feel it would change things," I said.

Kennet sighed. "I would be remiss not to tell you that this is not a wise move politically. I have no idea what the council's reaction will be, but I can't imagine that it will be positive."

"I understand," I said. Bugger the council and their reaction. My back ached with tension.

"As your adviser, I must caution you that you have surely made enemies during your time as a Seeker. The council will no longer be able to offer you protection should any of these people seek revenge."

I considered his words. It was true that making enemies was part of being a Seeker. Witches themselves, their friends and families—hardly anyone was glad when a Seeker came to call. But what kind of protection was the council able to provide? The council leaders were at odds with one another, working at cross-purposes. The council kept bungling things, kept making the easiest decision instead of the best one. I shook my head silently. There was no way I could rely on their protection anymore, anyway.

"I'll take my chances," I told Kennet.

"Gìomanach, as your mentor, I'm asking you to reconsider," he said cajolingly. "You are my protégé, the youngest Seeker the council has ever had. Please tell me you'll at least think more about this decision."

"No, Kennet," I said. "This is my final answer. I can no longer take part in what the council has become." It was very difficult for me, having to say this. In his day, before the council had started to slip out of hand, Kennet really had been an excellent mentor. I had relied on him a great deal during my first months as a Seeker. But things were different now.

"I can't tell you how disappointing this is to me personally, as it will be to the rest of the council," he said, the warmth in his voice leaching away. He didn't sound angry now so much as regretful and hurt.

"I realize that. But I know this is the right thing for me to do."

"I hope you'll give this further thought," he said, sounding stiff.

"Good-bye, Kennet."

Click. I looked at the phone in wonder. He'd hung up without saying good-bye. I hung up and pressed my eyes with the heels of my hands, trying to dispel tension. The conversation had been difficult—every bit as difficult as I'd feared, perhaps worse. But it was done. I had quit the council. I rolled my shoulders, feeling like a huge weight had been removed. I felt relieved but also frightened: I wasn't trained to do anything else.

Automatically I picked up my phone and rang Morgan. She'd been through the whole decision-making process with me. I knew talking to her now would definitely help. Talking to her always helped.

"Hello?" Not Morgan.

"Hi, Mrs. Rowlands," I said to Morgan's mother. "It's Hunter. Is Morgan there, please?"

"I'm sorry, Hunter—Morgan's taken her sister to a friend's house. Can I have her call you?"

"Yes, thanks—or I can catch her later. Good-bye, Mrs. Rowlands."

"Bye, Hunter."

I hung up and sighed. No immediate Morgan. I rubbed the back of my neck and settled down again, this time to gift some dried lavender with extra soothing properties.

"Hunter?"

I looked up to see Alyce, followed by two middle-aged women. One looked slightly older than the other, I'd guess in her late fifties. She was lean and muscled like a former dancer, with crisp silver hair cut in a simple style that just skimmed her jawline. She was wearing off-white canvas pants, loose but not sloppy, a trim T-shirt, and an unconstructed canvas jacket over that. Everything about her showed confidence, maturity, self-control, an acceptance of self.

The younger woman was a striking contrast. She was perhaps in her early forties but as surrounded by layers of agitation as the first seemed pared down to the essentials. Her layered, wispy skirt and top flowed around her in batiked shades of olive green and soft brown. She was slightly plump. Her heavy makeup was almost like icing.

Without thinking, I cast out my senses: Alyce was curious but not disturbed. The two women were blood witches. From them I got uncertainty, mistrust, even an edge of fear.

"Hunter, these women were asking for you," Alyce supplied. She turned to them and gestured to me. "Celia and Robin, this is Hunter Niall."

The two women exchanged glances, and then, as if making a decision, the older woman nodded. "Thank you, Alyce," she said. It was a gentle dismissal, and Alyce raised her eyebrows at me when they couldn't see her, then left.

I took a moment to examine them with ingrained Seeker thoroughness. They both had relatively weak energy patterns—they were blood witches, but not powerhouses.

The older woman stepped forward. "I'm Celia Evans," she said in a smooth, modulated voice. She held out her hand, and I rose to shake it. Her grip was firm but not aggressive. "And this is Robin Goodacre." She gestured to her companion, who then stepped forward. Where Celia projected calm and confidence, Robin projected a fluttery distraction that I instinctively felt came from insecurity, or nonacceptance of herself.

I shook Robin's hand. "Hello," she said, in a nervous, breathless voice. I wondered what her relationship was to Celia.

"Hello," I said. There were a couple of unmatched chairs in the corner, and I pulled them over, then sat down again at my table. I gestured for the two women to sit, and they did. "Can I help you with something?"

"Well, we've heard about you as a . . . uh . . ." Robin began, then seemed to get stymied by self-consciousness.

Celia took over. "We've come to see you because we've heard that you're—experienced with good magick and with . . . dark magick."

Hmmm. I nodded and waited for her to go on.

"Like the dark wave, for instance," Celia continued, beginning to seem slightly uncomfortable. "Or perhaps other kinds of dark magick."

Oh. Of course. "You need a Seeker?" I asked, and Robin visibly pulled back.

Celia looked alarmed. "We need . . . someone to help us. Someone who would recognize what might be dark magick. And maybe know what to do about it."

"Well, I'm sorry, but I no longer work for the council. I could put you in touch with someone, though."

"Actually," Celia said slowly, "we hadn't realized you were a Seeker. We wouldn't have come if we'd known. It's much better for us that you're *not* a Seeker, not part of the council.

Honestly, we need help, and we don't know where to find it."

Robin's plump hands fluttered around her skirt, playing with its folds. "It has to be the right kind of help," she said earnestly. "We can't make matters worse. But we don't know what to do." She twisted her hands together, her chunky rings clicking. "We heard you had experience with all kinds of things. We heard . . . you could be trusted."

That was interesting. I looked from Robin's round, earnest face, the distress in her brown eyes, to Celia's barely concealed tension.

"Can I ask who referred you to me?"

"Joanna Silversmith," said Celia. "Of Knotworthy. We went to school together."

Her name sounded familiar, but I didn't think I knew her personally. Knotworthy was a coven back in England, so maybe I had run across her there.

"Can you tell me a few more specifics about your problem?" I asked gently. "Then if I can't help you, maybe I'll know someone who can."

"It's our coven leader," Celia said, and took a deep breath. "We think she may be involved with dark magick."

3

Morgan

As I had done hundreds of times before, I parked my beloved Valiant, Das Boot, at the curb by my best friend Bree Warren's house and walked up the stone path to the double front doors. I rang the bell, and the door was opened almost instantly by Thalia Cutter, one of the other coven members. Our coven, Kithic, had the ideal number of members, thirteen: our leader and my boyfriend, Hunter Niall, Bree, Robbie Gurevitch, Sharon Goodfine, Ethan Sharp, Simon Bakehouse, Thalia, Jenna Ruiz, Raven Meltzer, Alisa Soto (our youngest member), Hunter's cousin, Sky, who was in England right now, Matt Adler, and me. I had known most of these people my whole life. Bree and Robbie had been my best friends since first grade. Sharon, Jenna, Matt, Ethan, and Alisa all went to my high school. Thalia and Simon went to the other high school in town.

"Hi," said Thalia. Her long, wavy hair hung almost to her waist, and her oval face was smooth and serene. "Come on in. Bree's in the kitchen. We're setting up in the pool house."

"Okay." From experience we'd found that at Bree's, the slate patio in her pool's enclosure was best for channeling energy. I headed for the kitchen and passed Ethan carrying a tall pillar candle. Bree called after him, "Wait—take a paper plate to put it on. If we get wax on the slate, we'll never get it off."

Ethan took the plate from her, smiled a greeting at me, and went out.

"Hi," I called, walking into the Warrens' huge kitchen. Bree, looking beautiful as usual, was arranging some cut fruit on a plate. Her fine, mink-dark hair had grown out a bit and fell in feathery layers past her shoulders. I sighed. It wasn't easy being best friends with someone who looked like a model. We're talking high cheekbones, fabulous body, the works. Always impossibly, sophisticatedly hip, she was wearing an Indian-print cotton skirt that hung several inches below her belly button and a white peasant top that showed perfect, ivory skin both above and below.

I tried not to look down at my own lame ensemble of jeans and T-shirt. I was just about to start feeling bummed when I remembered Hunter—incredibly hot and irresistible Hunter—and the fact that he didn't seem able to keep his hands off me.

"Look—Bree's making food from scratch," said Robbie, cutting up fresh pineapple at one end of the Corian counter.

"Oh, so *witty*," said Bree, but she smiled at him, and he smiled back. It was obvious how strongly they felt about each other. She went back to artistically placing strawberries on the platter.

"That looks great," I said, inhaling the tropical scent of pineapple, heavy in the air. Now that spring had finally sprung, I was relishing the lighter clothes, the warmer weather, the longer days. It had been a long, dark winter, in more ways than one. I was looking forward to being in the light again.

"Hi," said Alisa, entering the kitchen. Her wavy, caramel-streaked hair was pulled back off her face, emphasizing her huge dark eyes. "Can I help with anything?"

"Thanks, I think we're about ready," Bree said. "As soon as everyone's here, we can start."

Alisa and I trailed out of the kitchen. We'd had kind of an up-and-down relationship in the months since Kithic had formed. Things had been difficult for Alisa lately. She had recently found out that she was half blood witch on her mother's side, which had really freaked her out. A few weeks ago she'd run away, partly to find her late mother's family in Gloucester, a family of full blood witches. The trip had wreaked havoc on her home life—her dad had had a fit—but in some way it seemed that she had found what she was looking for. These days she seemed happier, more centered. I don't know whether she was doing dances of joy over being a blood witch, but she seemed to have accepted it.

"How's it going?" I asked her in the hallway. The last circle that Alisa had attended had been a little strange. She had been stressed out, and since she had trouble controlling her powers, that stress had made all of the faucets in Hunter's house spew uncontrollably. Eventually his house had practically flooded. She had been really upset.

"Not too bad," she said. "Things are a tiny bit better at home—Hilary's stopped barfing, so that's good. And get this—she's quit calling me the flower girl. I'm now a real bridesmaid."

"Way to go," I said, and we both grinned. Her father was marrying his pregnant girlfriend soon. Hilary was only about ten years older than Alisa, and they'd had a really rocky start. But it sounded like her stepmother-to-be was getting more sensitive.

"At least she's trying," Alisa said, "and I've been trying, too. Not that it's easy. But she agreed to alter my dress so I won't have that huge bow across my butt anymore."

"Excellent," I said. We'd stopped beneath a weird abstract oil painting right outside Mr. Warren's home office. "What about your room?"

"Dad's buying me a new bed for my new room," Alisa reported. Hilary had made her move out of her old room so she could be closer to the baby. "Oh, you know, Dad said I could invite a guest to the wedding."

"Hmmm, like Charlie of Gloucester?" I said, raising my eyebrows suggestively. Alisa smiled and looked a little embarrassed. One of the people Alisa had met in Gloucester was Charlie, a member of her mother's family's coven and a cute, funny, attractive blood witch. He and Alisa kept up through e-mail.

"No," Alisa whispered. "I'm sure Charlie wouldn't be able to come all this way. But I want Mary K. to come—I've called her twice, but she's never home."

And she obviously hadn't returned Alisa's calls. My sister was still pretty uncomfortable with the whole Wicca/blood witch thing, though she seemed to have accepted it as far as I was concerned. Maybe finding out that her best friend was some kind of weird, witchy creature, in addition to her sister, was just too much for her. Mary K.'d been really upset when Alisa had discovered her heritage. I hoped she wouldn't give up on their friendship.

"She's been seeing Mark Chambers a lot lately," I said neutrally. "But I'll remind her."

"Thanks."

Matt passed us on the way to the pool house and said hey, and then Raven stomped down the hallway in her Doc Martens. She was wearing a vintage rayon dress with huge gaps held together by safety pins. This, her cornrowed black hair, and her clunky shoes added up to a picture that was totally Raven.

Then the back of my neck tingled, and a whole cascade of responses, emotional and physical, burst through me like sparks. My head was already swiveling as Hunter said, "Morgan?"

He was standing at the foyer entrance to the hall. Alisa melted away toward the pool, and I tried not to run and fling myself into Hunter's arms. I'd spoken to him just before dinner, and he'd told me that he'd finally truly quit the council. I was dying to talk to him. Among other things.

"Hi," I said, walking toward him, admiring my incredible self-restraint. He came to meet me halfway, and then my restraint broke loose. I put my arms around him, backed down the hallway, and drew him into Mr. Warren's office. With the door shut behind us, I let my huge, goofy smile show. He drew me closer, smiling also, and then he bent down and I went on tiptoe to meet his kiss. I pressed closer to him, molding myself against his lean body, feeling the strength of his arms as he held me tightly. My hand reached up to touch the short, light blond hair at the back of his neck, and my fingers traced the smoothness of the skin there. Hunter. Everything about him spoke to me. The timbre of his voice, the scent of his skin, the depth of his green eyes. The way his jaw tightened and his eyes narrowed when he was angry. The sound of his breathing when we were making out on his bed. The pressure of his hand as he splayed his fingers across my back, urging me closer. His quirky, dry sense of humor. His incredible intelligence. His strong and controlled magick. I admired and respected him. I felt incredibly tender love and incredibly strong desire for him. I trusted him implicitly. I shivered as Hunter pushed his knee between my legs. I coiled one leg around his as we kept kissing each other over and over, as if we'd been separated for a year instead of a day. I wanted to drink him in, imprint him on my skin, be warmed by his touch.

Eventually we slowed and came up for air. My lips felt swollen, and I was breathing hard. Hunter's eyes glittered down at me.

"Well, hello to you, too," he said in his soft English accent. "Did you miss me?"

I grinned and nodded slowly. "Just a little. But enough about me. Tell me everything that happened with Kennet."

Hunter shook his head and let out a breath. "I told him I was quitting. He said witches don't quit the council. I said I did. He asked if I'd consider it a leave of absence. I said I quit. He said I would no longer have the council's protection and that I had made a lot of enemies, being a Seeker."

"Nice," I said with a grimace. "Glad he was so understanding and supportive."

He shrugged. "He wasn't bad, really. I suppose he didn't know what to do."

I stood close to him and rested my head against his chest. I heard the strong, steady beat of his heart. "I'm sorry," I said. "But how do you feel about it? Are you glad you did it?"

"I don't think I should reconsider," Hunter said, stroking my back. "I gave quitting a lot of thought. I know it's right for me."

I leaned up and kissed his cheek. "We should probably get back to the others, but if you want to talk about this more later, we should, okay?" I asked.

He nodded, his chin against the top of my head. His fingers trailed smoothly down my shirt.

"Where's Morgan?" I heard Sharon say out in the hall. "Didn't you say she was here? Isn't Hunter coming?"

We waited until the hallway was quiet, then slipped out. I ducked into the powder room, and Hunter headed to the pool house as if he'd just gotten here. Quickly I splashed water on my face, seeing the flush of Hunter's kisses there. Then I pushed my brown hair off my shoulders and went to join the others.

"Welcome, everyone," Hunter was saying as I walked out onto the enclosed patio that surrounded Bree's pool. Dim stars shone overheard through the tinted glass ceiling, and Bree, with her usual flair, had arranged perhaps fifty pillar candles of various heights all along one edge of the pool. Their flames were reflected in the dark water and provided our only light. The effect was beautiful and mysterious.

Several people turned to greet me silently, and I smiled and nodded, then took a place between Jenna and Raven.

"Bree, thanks for hosting," Hunter said. "It's always nice to be here."

"No problem," said Bree.

"Now, before we cast our circle tonight, does anyone have any announcements or questions?" Hunter asked. "Where are we meeting next time?"

"It can be at my house," Simon offered.

"Right, cheers," said Hunter. "Since we're coming up on Beltane, the next official circle won't be for a while. But in the meantime, we have one of our most festive celebrations to look forward to. Have you guys read about it?"

"Yes," said Thalia. "It's a fire festival, and with Samhain, it's one of the most important Sabbats."

"Right," said Hunter. "Like Samhain, Beltane takes place when the veils between the worlds are the thinnest. At Samhain we celebrate and honor death and endings, the closing of a circle, the end of a cycle. Beltane, the last of all the spring fertility festivals, is all about birth, new beginnings, life. Traditionally people make bonfires, have maypoles, and celebrate all night. It's when the Goddess, ripe with fertility after the long winter, joins again with the God, who has now grown into manhood."

There were a few somewhat embarrassed giggles at this, and Hunter acknowledged them with a grin. "This is when the Goddess conceives the next God and so propagates the life cycle once again. Does anyone know the symbols of Beltane?"

I did, but I didn't say anything. My covenmates knew that Hunter and I were going out. I usually stayed pretty quiet at circles—I didn't want to be seen as the teacher's pet. When Hunter was in Canada and Bethany Malone had led our circles, I had been more outspoken.

"The maypole," said Robbie, and Bree raised her eyebrows suggestively, making people laugh.

"Doesn't it have some of the same symbols as Ostara?" asked Sharon. "Like bunnies and eggs?"

Hunter nodded. "Symbols of fertility."

"I read where people actually have sex outside, to bless their fields or their animals," Raven said.

Hunter laughed. "Well, that's one tradition we don't have to feel obliged to perform."

I saw Bree and Robbie exchange glances, Sharon and Ethan making faces at each other, Jenna and Simon smiling quietly and looking at their feet. Jeez, had all of them already done it? Was I the only seventeen-year-old virgin left in Widow's Vale? Hunter and I had planned to make love a couple of times, but something had always happened to keep us from going through with it. Now we both knew that we were ready—we were just waiting for the time to be right. I hoped it would be right very soon.

"Before our next circle," Hunter went on, "I'd like all of you to do some more reading about Beltane." He listed some useful sources, then said, "Now, if there's nothing else, we can cast our circle."

We stepped forward. Hunter quickly and expertly drew a perfect circle on the slates with a piece of chalk. We went in through the opening he'd left in it, and then he closed it behind us. We'd set up four bowls, one each at east, north, west, and south. They held dirt, to symbolize earth, a smoldering incense cone to symbolize air, a candle for fire, and water. With the four elements represented, our energy would be balanced.

The twelve of us joined hands, and Hunter said, "I invoke the Goddess. I invoke the God. I invite them to join us at this our circle. Tonight we celebrate being together, being at the threshold of spring. As we raise the Goddess's energy, we'll think about our own renewals, rebirths. Now, everyone can join in when they're ready." We began to move our circle deasil, or clockwise, as Hunter began singing a familiar power chant.

One by one we blended our voices with his, letting the words weave together. I waited for just a few moments, and then it happened, as it always did: I felt a burst of happiness, of joy. I knew who I was, I knew what I was doing. I was joining my energy with that of others, and it was an incredible experience.

As we moved more quickly, our feet keeping pace with the complex, ancient rhythm, I gradually began to be aware of another thread of sound underneath the one we were singing. It was inside my head, coming from within, and I followed it like a colored string, trying to untangle it. It was elusive, not complete, and I couldn't seem to get closer to it. Sometimes it seemed vaguely familiar, but I just couldn't place where I'd ever heard it. Still, I moved with the others in a circle, one part of my mind focused on the thread. Vague images came to me: when my half brother Killian had used a hawk's true name to force it to earth and also, weirdly, when my biological father, Ciaran MacEwan, had initiated me into the racking pains and heady pleasures of shape-shifting. But these thoughts drifted away like clouds, and soon my mind was full of the excitement of our raised energy. My heart felt both full and light, my vision seemed exceptionally clear—I could see the faint, colorful auras shimmering around my friends' heads. Being part of a circle was like plugging myself into a higher consciousness, a higher reality. It was completely fulfilling.

Our pace quickened, and our chanting swelled to bursting.

Our joined energy rose and crested, and at the peak of its crescendo we flung our hands apart and stopped where we were. Smiles on our faces, our hands floating downward, we looked around to enjoy the looks of transport on one another's faces.

My gaze locked on Hunter, on his angular, fair-skinned face, his sharp cheekbones, the amazing depth of his eyes. His cheeks were flushed with a pale pink, like dawn breaking. His eyes met mine, and between us there flashed an instant understanding, an immediate message of love sent and received. I smiled, and he returned it.

"That was a great circle, everyone," he said, assuming his leadership role again. "I can see a definite improvement in your focus and concentration."

I remembered the elusive tune and the strange images I'd seen in the circle. Why had I thought of shape-shifting again? Was the Goddess trying to tell me something? Or was it just that now that we were out of immediate danger, my mind was really beginning to deal with those images? Probably the latter, I decided. There had been no new or scary information in the images.

"I've got some food and stuff in the kitchen," Bree said, brushing her fine hair off her face. "Robbie and I will get it."

Hunter drifted over to me as they left, and automatically our arms went around each other's waist. He kissed the top of my head, and I shivered. All thoughts of the elusive tune I'd heard had disappeared. I'd meant to mention the strange dream I'd had to Hunter but decided not to. Everyone has weird dreams sometimes.

4

Hunter

"What about here?" I asked. "No rocks, a mixture of sun and shade, nice view." The picnic basket was starting to feel heavy—I was ready to sit and eat and lie in the sun.

"This looks good," Morgan agreed, nodding.

"Okay by me," said Robbie.

For a moment it looked like Bree might object, but then she followed majority rule. She and Morgan unfolded an old blanket and shook it out.

"Goddess, what a beautiful day," Morgan said, immediately lying down on the blanket in a way that made me wish Robbie and Bree weren't there. I wanted to touch her, feel the smooth skin of her stomach. Well, nothing I could do about it yet.

By unspoken agreement the four of us ended up on our backs, looking up at the intensely blue spring sky and the puffy white clouds slipping past.

"This is great," Robbie said.

"Mmm," Bree murmured in agreement. "Oh, Morgan, did

I tell you? That B and B on Martha's Vineyard worked out."

"Hey, great," Morgan said. "When are you guys going?"

"The end of June," Robbie said. "Just for a week. I don't think I'll be able to get more time off from the shop." Robbie had gotten a summer job at Widow's Vale's tiny used-book store.

Using my lightning-fast former Seeker intuition, I deduced that Bree and Robbie were going to Martha's Vineyard together for a week later in the summer. A quiet envy settled across me. I would *kill* to have that kind of time alone with Morgan. Sometimes I wished her father were more like Bree's father—rather absent and not entirely aware of what she did. I knew that Morgan's intensely caring and involved parents were, in general, a much better thing. But sometimes . . .

"That sounds so great," Morgan said. "I'm probably going to be working at my mom's office all summer. Data entry, filing, et cetera. Making coffee. Yawn." Her mom was a real estate agent, and I knew Morgan often worked for her when she needed money.

"At least you'll be in air-conditioning," Bree pointed out. "Which reminds me—speaking of being chilly—I was reading about Beltane online this morning, and it seems that many covens feel the Beltane rites are best done skyclad. Like the fertility rites, the dances. The maypole."

"Skyclad?" Robbie asked. "What does that—*oh*."

Bree giggled and crossed one of her legs over Robbie's.

"I'm so sure," Morgan said, rolling her eyes. "Count me out."

Trying not to laugh, I said, "I don't know, Morgan. I believe that if we're going to be historically accurate, Kithic should celebrate Beltane authentically. I imagine it would be all right if not *everyone* has sex under the moon, but the nudity . . . pfaw!" I stopped to spit some grass, which Morgan had been flinging at me, out of my mouth and held up my hands to ward off any further attacks.

"Very funny," said Morgan, throwing more grass. I half sat up to brush it off and saw that her face was flushed with self-consciousness. I grinned at her. In public she was fairly reserved, and she certainly didn't dress to show off her body. But in private . . . we had been together enough for me to know that her physical desire and innate sensuality ran as strong in her as her magickal powers did. And I had been the lucky recipient of those feelings. I hoped that soon we would be ready to take those feelings to their natural conclusion.

"Right, then," I said, lying back down and grabbing Morgan's hand. I held her hand on my chest and felt her relax against me, her foot resting against my ankle. "So I'll go ahead and inform the coven that nudity and public sex are optional."

Robbie snorted with laughter, and Bree told him, "You can strip down first."

I was happy, lying there in the sun and dappled shade. It felt normal, natural, light. I hoped that the rest of the year would be more like this and that the darkness we'd been facing had finally gone for good.

After a while we sat up and ate our sandwiches. Everything tasted better because we were outside in the cool spring sun and we were together. I lay on my back with Morgan and her friends and watched the clouds. I couldn't remember the last time I'd felt this calm.

Not long after that, Bree and Robbie took their leave to make a foreign-film matinee in Taunton. Bree left the dessert with us, and soon we heard the distinctive sound of her BMW driving off. Leaving me alone with Morgan at last.

I turned on my side and gathered her to me, pushing her down on the blanket with my weight, feeling her slenderness beneath me, her leg automatically bending to curve around mine. Her arms came around me and I began kissing her all over, touching her everywhere. I felt intensely alive, curious, excited about our future. My body responded to hers so strongly that I knew if we waited much longer to make love, both of us would lose our minds. It wasn't until I felt her hand on mine that I realized I was at her waist and I had undone the button on her jeans.

Feeling foggy, I blinked and looked at her flushed face. I looked down at my hand and at her hand holding it. She smiled at me with slow amusement.

"Right here? Wouldn't we scare the chipmunks?"

I was too far gone to make a coherent response right away. Everything in me was telling me to charge ahead, and the fact that we had stopped and she was talking was taking a while to imprint on my lust-clouded brain.

"Mommy, what are those huge ugly animals doing?" Morgan said in a high, squeaky chipmunk voice. "Don't look, sweetie," she answered in a concerned mother chipmunk voice. "Just go back in the tree."

For a moment I just stared at her, then I started laughing hard. Morgan grinned at me while I guffawed, and it was only with effort that I got my wits about me. Leaning down, I kissed her on the nose. "You are incredibly odd," I said tenderly. "Really, incredibly odd. I'm sure that's the first time in the history of human sexuality that someone has imitated a chipmunk as part of foreplay."

We laughed together then, sitting up and holding on to each other, cackling like maniacs. She rebuttoned her jeans, and when we lay back down again, it was just to cuddle and talk. In the back of my mind I remembered my upcoming meeting with Celia Evans and Robin Goodacre. All they'd told me was that they were concerned about their coven leader possibly working dark magick. They weren't sure what to do but needed help in deciding if there was anything they *could* do. Later tonight we were going to meet again, and they'd promised to give me the whole story.

I had wanted to talk to Morgan about them, get her impressions on what she thought might be going on. But I didn't have their permission to talk to anyone, and while I would have felt all right about telling another Wiccan "professional," like my da, telling Morgan seemed like a breach of confidence.

"What are you going to do this summer?" Morgan asked me, snuggling close, and I heard the wistfulness in her voice. She was thinking of Bree and Robbie's trip, no doubt.

"Well, I'm hoping to earn enough money to go home for a while," I told her honestly. "I want to see everyone, eat some decent fish and chips, fill up on England." She was quiet, playing thoughtfully with one of my shirt buttons, and I went on. "Is there any way you could go with me? What about if you promise to visit historical sites and write a report?"

She smiled, looking sad. "I'll ask my parents, but don't hold your breath."

I cuddled her closer again. We both knew, without saying it, that there was no way her parents would let her go to Europe with a guy. Not when she was only seventeen. I nuzzled her beneath one ear and felt her shiver. "We need time alone." Morgan nodded. "Then maybe we could get around to certain things we've been thinking about," I said meaningfully. Her hazel eyes, the color of stones seen through clear water, brightened with amusement, and she gave an instinctive wiggle against me. I kissed her gently, not wanting us to get all worked up again. Soon we were lying still again, our arms around each other, looking up at the sky.

As my eyes drifted lazily closed, I heard an odd cry above me. My eyes fluttered open and my gaze fastened on a red-tailed hawk, shooting groundward incredibly fast. It dropped below the level of the trees but almost instantly shot upward, each strong beat of its powerful wings taking it farther into the sky. In its talons was a writhing black snake.

"Lunch," I said, admiring the bird's almost perfect predatory ability. I looked down to see Morgan frowning.

"That's weird," she said, squinting to watch the bird disappear high above us.

"Why? Hawks hunt all the time. This place is full of red-tailed hawks." I stroked her hair, loving the way the sunlight played across it.

"Yeah, I guess," Morgan said slowly. "It's nothing."

"I have to tell you," I said, gently easing her head up onto my shoulder, "I'm not thrilled about working at Practical Magick."

"No?"

I shook my head. "I know I can't be a Seeker anymore, but putting little spells on herbs isn't my life's calling, either. If only—it would be so great if the council weren't the only show in town."

"What do you mean?" Morgan asked, rolling over on her side and tucking one arm under her head so she could look at me.

"Well, if there were an alternate council, say," I said. "One that held more closely to the Wiccan Rede."

Morgan was quiet for a moment, and I wondered if she understood what I was feeling. "Maybe you should start your own council," she said.

I laughed, then saw that she looked solemn and thoughtful. "You're not serious." The idea of me creating a whole new council, single-handedly, was laughable. "Are you?"

"How serious are *you*?" she asked me, and I had no answer.

I was almost out the front door that evening when the phone rang. I debated not answering it—I had only ten minutes to get to the coffee shop where I was meeting Celia and Robin—but then I picked up on the fact that it was Sky calling. I lunged for the phone.

"Hello-ello," I said, and she snorted. "How's jolly olde England?"

"Still repressed as ever," Sky said dryly. "Even English witches are more restrained than American ones."

"You say that like it's a bad thing," I said, and she allowed herself an amused heh-heh.

"I guess it *is* a bit of a relief not to have everyone's emotions hanging out all over," she said. "On the other hand, Americans seem simpler to deal with. They say what they feel or think, and you never have to guess what's going on behind the silence."

I thought for a moment, and it came to me. "How's Uncle Beck?"

Sky sighed loudly into the phone, which told me I'd hit my mark. As light and beautiful and loving as my mum had been, her brother, Beck, Sky's father, was dark and hard hewn and almost forcefully introverted. He'd raised me, my younger brother, Linden, and my sister, Alwyn, from the time I was eight, and though I'd always felt physically safe and taken care of, I'd also always felt wary, distanced, and on thin ice emotionally. Sky and her four sisters hadn't fared much better, though they were his own daughters.

"Anyway, I think I'm ready to come back to Widow's Vale," she said.

"Good news," I said sincerely. "It's not the same without you."

"Right. So I think I'm getting a standby flight, probably on Tuesday. Think you can give me a lift home if I tell you when?"

"Absolutely," I said. "Why standby?"

"It'll be cheaper," she said, "and I can't see waiting another two weeks for a discounted flight."

So the family was definitely getting on her nerves. She'd stuck it out for a long while, though. "Just give me some advance notice and I'll be there," I promised.

"Cheers. Anything happening?"

"Yeah, Da is more in demand—" I broke off as I caught sight of the clock. "Damn! I'm sorry, Sky—I'm late for a meeting. I'll talk to you later, all right?"

"Sure. 'Bye."

I hung up the phone and raced out the door.

"Sorry I'm late," I said as I arrived at the coffee shop almost fifteen minutes later. Celia looked up at me, then glanced at her watch. I got the message. She was dressed as though she'd come from an office, in neat, tailored navy pants and jacket that looked professional yet not too formal or uncomfortable.

"I had an international phone call just as I was leaving the house," I explained truthfully, sliding into the remaining seat at our small table.

Robin glanced at Celia, and when I focused my senses, I picked up on feelings of nervousness, fear, and guilt. Once again I found myself intrigued. What was it they wanted, exactly?

"Why don't you get something to drink and then we'll talk," Celia suggested. I nodded and went to the counter. While I waited for my tea, I looked around the small café. Only one other table was occupied. Celia and Robin had chosen a table in the far corner, and each of them was sitting with her back to a wall.

I carried my huge cup over and sat down. I stirred in two packets of sugar and waited for one of the witches to speak. They kept glancing at each other, as if communicating telepathically, but they weren't, I didn't think. I waited, trying to look unconcerned. People want to talk. I'd found that out as a Seeker. Simply waiting was often a far more effective means of getting information than a hard-edged interrogation.

"Thank you for coming," Celia said at last. "When you were late, we wondered if you'd changed your mind."

"No," I said mildly, talking a sip of tea. "I would have called."

"We need you to promise you won't do anything without our permission," Robin blurted, an anxious look on her round face.

I met her gaze calmly. "Why don't you just explain what's going on?"

Celia leaned forward, the smooth planes of her face taut with tension. "Can we *trust* you?" she asked, her voice low and intent.

"Do you practice dark magick?" I asked, and she drew back.

"No," she said in surprise.

"Then you can trust me." I took another big sip.

"It isn't *us*," Robin said. There was so much anxiety coming off her that I was starting to feel jumpy myself. I kept casting out my senses to be aware of any possible danger nearby. But there was nothing.

"You said it was your coven leader," I said.

"Yes, and we need you to promise that you won't . . . harm her," Robin went on. Celia gave her a sharp glance, and Robin looked down and began twisting her hands together in her lap.

"I would never harm anyone," I said. "Unless they posed a threat." I couldn't figure out what these two were getting at. Of course, if I found a witch practicing dark magick that might hurt someone, I had an obligation to turn them in to the council to have their power stripped. As little faith as I had in the council these days, I still knew how important it was to prevent anyone from causing harm.

Robin glanced at Celia nervously, and the two of them seemed to be considering my reply. Finally Celia looked around as if to make sure we were alone. Then her clear brown eyes met mine. "We're both members of Willowbrook, a mixed coven up in Thornton."

Thornton was a town about forty minutes away, north and east from Widow's Vale. A mixed coven meant that not only was it blood witches and nonblood witches, but also blood witches of different clans. I was sure Willowbrook had been mentioned casually by people I'd talked to, but nothing in my memory triggered any negative reaction.

I nodded. "Go on."

Celia continued in a low tone. "For the last seventeen years Willowbrook has been led by a gifted Brightendale named Patrice Pearson."

"How long have you each been in the coven?" I asked. I had been around them enough now to realize that though they seemed to know each other well, there was a distance between them. They were covenmates but not best friends, and they certainly weren't lovers.

"Eighteen years," Celia answered.

"Twelve," said Robin.

"And there's a problem?" I asked.

"Patrice is wonderful," Robin said earnestly, leaning closer to me. Her round brown eyes were once again surrounded by complicated makeup.

"But . . ." I said leadingly, and Celia looked annoyed.

"But nothing," she said shortly. "Patrice *is* wonderful. She's so . . . warm. Giving, helpful, caring, full of joy and life." She paused. "I went through a very difficult personal situation a few years ago, and I don't know what I would have done without Patrice."

"We all just love her so much," Robin said. "We're all so close as a coven. Most of us have been together for at least ten years or more. Patrice just brings us closer and makes us all feel—" She looked for the word. "Loved. Even— About six years ago Patrice went through an ugly divorce. We were all so surprised. But even through all that, she came to circle each week without fail. Every week. And led our circle with generosity and joy."

"She's an exceptional leader," Celia said simply. "She has exceptional clarity and focus." I was starting to get a bad feeling about the perfect Patrice.

"But lately," Celia said, and she and Robin exchanged glances one more time. "Lately she's been different."

I relaxed in my chair. Now that the dam had been breached, everything else would follow. I projected feelings of calm, of being nonjudgmental.

"She's unchanged in most ways, but sometimes—it's almost as if someone else is looking out through her eyes."

All my senses went on alert.

"Circles are different, too," said Robin. "They've always been the high point of my week. Energizing. Life affirming."

"But lately several of us have noticed that after circles, we feel unusually drained," Celia said, looking at her long, slim fingers wrapped around her mug. "Sometimes some of us have to lie down afterward. One night a few weeks ago Robin and I finally mentioned it to each other and found we were feeling the same things. So we decided to try to find help. *Discreet* help. We can't say what's wrong or even *if* anything's wrong. But it doesn't feel completely right anymore, either."

"Of course, Patrice has been under an awful lot of pressure," Robin said. "Joshua—her son, he's eleven now—was diagnosed last year with leukemia. He underwent a bone-marrow transplant about eight months ago."

"Now he has host-versus-graft disease," Celia went on.

"What's that?" I asked.

"Well, they matched Joshua up with a donor," Celia said. "Then they did massive chemo and radiation to kill all the cancer-causing cells. It killed all of Joshua's own bone marrow, too.

Then the donor's cancer-free marrow was implanted in him. It's working, in that it's producing white blood cells and boosting his immune system. Unfortunately, this marrow's white blood cells have identified Joshua himself as being foreign, and the marrow is attacking virtually every system in his body."

Her voice was tight with pain, and I reflected on the fact that both of these women must have known Patrice when Joshua was first born and had probably known about or been involved in his upbringing for the last eleven years. Now he was deathly ill. It wasn't only Patrice who was feeling the strain.

"It's a different kind of sickness from the cancer," Celia said. "But still awful. It could kill him."

"He's in such pain, such misery," Robin said, her voice wavering. "But even with all this, Patrice has missed only two or three circles in the past year."

"I offered to take over leading the circles for a while, to give her a break," said Celia. "I'm the most senior member of the coven. But she refused."

"That's how loyal she is, how dedicated," Robin said.

"What do the other coven members say?" I asked.

"I know some of them feel something's wrong," said Celia. "No one's said anything to me outright. The thing is, every once in a while it seems fine. It almost made me wonder if I was just imagining things or coming down with the flu myself."

"But I felt all the same things," Robin said. "And last week I heard someone else whisper a concern about it."

"If something negative is affecting all the coven members . . . we have to figure out what," Celia said firmly.

"We know Patrice is a good person," Robin put in quickly. "We just think she needs help, maybe."

I frowned, sipping my tea. This did not sound good. Of course, there might be some benign, rational explanation. And it would be wonderful if that were true. But instinctively I felt there was more to this.

"What is it you want me to do?" I asked carefully.

"We want you to . . . figure out what's going on," Celia said, and Robin nodded. "As a former Seeker, you would have investigative skills, knowledge about the different paths witches take, ideas about how to confront Patrice if it's necessary."

"If she's strayed a little, we can help her get back on the right path," Robin said.

"Or maybe just figure out how to protect her from herself," Celia suggested. "Or protect us from her. We don't know, really. We just know we need help."

"And we need to keep this very, very quiet," Robin said urgently. "We don't want you to go to the council, even if you have affiliations. Patrice is a good person. She just needs help."

I rubbed my chin while I thought. "I don't know whether I can promise that. If I discover that Patrice is involved in something dangerous . . . I'm no longer a Seeker, but I still have an obligation, as a blood witch with a conscience." I leaned back, and Celia and Robin both seemed to deflate a bit.

"Well . . ." Robin glanced at Celia hesitantly.

"We don't . . . we don't want anyone to be hurt," Celia assured me. "Perhaps . . . what if you make no promises, except that you won't harm anybody unnecessarily and you won't let anyone else be harmed?"

I sighed and considered her words. Well, at the very least, I could certainly track down more answers than they had now. "That goes without saying. Maybe I can look into it," I agreed. "See what I can come up with. But if Patrice is mixed up in something dangerous—I simply can't let her continue."

Celia nodded tightly. "Of course. We just—"

"If there's another option other than calling in the council, we want to explore it," Robin said, nervously picking at a loose thread on her sleeve. "You know, we don't want to see her . . . hurt."

"Nobody wants to see anyone hurt," I assured her.

The two women sat back, relief emanating from them like perfume.

Blimey, I thought. What kind of mess have I gotten myself into?

5

Morgan

I'm in a huge house, huge like the palace of Versailles. I keep running down corridors, sure I know the way out, but no matter where I go, I only end up in more corridors, more halls, more rooms that lead nowhere. I feel like something's after me—I'm running away from something, but I don't know what or who. I'm cold, and my bare feet make no sound on the smooth floors. Several times I stop to look out a window, to try to get my bearings, maybe see someone who could help me. Each time I see dream walls floating outside, like stage scenery. They're scrawled over with runes, sigils, words, and magickal drawings, drawings that frighten me, even though I don't know what they are. Then I look out a window and see a hawk swooping down to attack. I don't know why, but this sight chills me to the very bone.

I begin to run down the corridors again. As I pass each enormous window, curtains burst into flames behind me. Is this house going to burn down with me in it? I need to get out of here, to escape. I'm so alone, so cold, so scared. Why can't I find my way out? What's after me? What's that dark, horrible shadow? The fire is crackling behind me, more shadows flickering on the walls ahead of me. I'm going to burn.

I woke myself up yelling something like, *Goddess, help me!* I was in my bed, sweating and clammy and icy all at the same time. I wondered if I had shouted out loud, but no one came to check, so I guessed I hadn't. I felt panicky and kept looking at my windows to make sure my shades weren't on fire. I drank some water in the bathroom and lay back down on my bed. I stared at the ceiling until the sun came up, and then I went back to sleep until it was time to meet everyone for the day's picnic.

That was last night. I had considered telling Hunter about it at our picnic, but suddenly it seemed so silly. Obviously I've been through a lot of stress lately. Who wouldn't have weird dreams?

This night will be different, I promised myself. I was trying to quiet whatever demons I was carrying around in my mind. I had taken a relaxing bath. I was trying to think good thoughts, to concentrate on positive things.

It was ten-thirty. I had reviewed some of my history notes in preparation for finals, figuring if that didn't put me to a sound sleep, nothing would.

"Good night, honey," Mom said, poking her head in my open door.

"Night, Mom," I said. I heard Mary K. brushing her teeth in the bathroom we shared, and I turned off my light, taking comfort in the familiar sounds. I thrashed around until I was comfortable and in the perfect Morgan sleeping position. *Now for good thoughts.*

The day had been so great. I'd gone on a picnic with

Hunter, Bree, and Robbie—my three favorite people. Bree and I had never been able to double-date before; though she'd always had boyfriends, I hadn't. And Bree and Robbie's relationship seemed to be going well. I'd never seen either of them so happy.

Okay, I thought. Good thoughts. The picnic had been perfect. And it had gotten only better after Bree and Robbie had taken off. I smiled to myself, thinking about Hunter and me. Goddess, he made me crazy. When, *when* could we be alone together the way we wanted—when would we finally make love?

Sometimes I felt so much love for Hunter that it overwhelmed me and I felt like I was going to cry. He was such a good person, such an ethical person. Such an incredibly talented, knowledgeable witch. I was totally fascinated by everything about him.

I was getting sleepy, and I felt warm and calm. I consciously relaxed every muscle in my body, starting from my toes and working my way up to the top of my head. I repeated my simple little soothing spell: Everything is fine and bright. Day must follow every night. My power keeps me safe from harm, and the Goddess holds me in her arms.

Then I fell asleep.

Frowning, I look down at the map spread out on the bench seat next to me. I squint, but all the names and roads and markings are blurred. Frustrated, I look through the windshield at the tree-lined road, hoping that some feature of it will become familiar. I shift into third gear, as if moving faster will help me feel less lost. I don't know where I am or where I'm going. I feel sure that I did know when I set out—but the reasoning escapes me now.

Das Boot feels familiar and comforting, moving heavily down the narrow road, but that's the only thing that feels okay. There are gray clouds ahead of me, low and malevolent in the sky, as if a storm is coming. I want to turn and go home but don't know which direction to turn in. And there are no cross streets, anyway—nowhere to turn.

Dammit. I look down at my map again, trying to force some of the symbols into focus. They're in Gaelic. I recognize a few letters, but none of them make sense. I feel so frustrated, I want to cry. What's wrong with me? I feel so stupid. The seconds slide by and I become more and more anxious, almost panicky. How can I fix this situation?

A sudden hard tap on my back windshield startles me. Carefully, trying not to drive off the road, I turn around to look—and almost scream. A huge, horrible, dark-feathered hawk is on the trunk of my car, its talons scraping paint as it holds on. Its hard golden eyes seem to laser right through me. It looks fierce and hateful and without pity.

I spin around again, ready to stomp on the gas to try to dislodge it, but instead find that I'm now a passenger in the car. Someone else is driving, and I keep trying to see who, but for some reason, whenever I try to look, I can never quite see all the way to the driver's side. Again and again I try, and my gaze keeps sliding away from where the driver is sitting. I can see in front of it and in back of it but not actually the driver's seat itself. Who is this? Am I being kidnapped? A burst of anxiety closes my throat.

A dim gray figure up ahead catches my eye, and I peer at it through my window. Can I signal this person for help? Huge, fat raindrops begin to pelt the windshield like tiny bullets, smacking forcefully against the glass. I lean forward to see who the shape is. I gasp in shock—it's Hunter! Stop! I cry, stop! but the car doesn't even slow down. I see Hunter's face, his eyes locking onto mine, his surprise and concern as we whiz by.

I bang on my window and turn around to yell back at him—I want to stop! I want to come get you, I can't! Tears of fear and anguish roll down my cheeks. I'm trapped in this car. I need to escape, need to get back to Hunter. Goddess, now I feel awful. I'm angry and in tears and so confused and powerless. I keep thinking, I want to stop, I want to stop, I want to stop.

Up ahead, the road begins a slow curve to the left. Das Boot slows, and impulsively I throw open my door and fling myself from the car. I hear the squeal of brakes, and then I'm rolling down a short embankment covered with sharp-thorned thistles. I tumble to a halt. My arms and legs are scratched, rain is pelting my face and hair, and cautiously I begin to climb toward the road, both hoping Das Boot and its mystery driver are gone and feeling upset that my car might be missing.

But there's something—I feel a warmth on my back. I feel back there with my hand, and I jump back—fire! I look behind me, and there are wings made of fire flowing from my back! Who *am I?* What *am I?*

No car is on the road. Evening is sweeping in like a cape, flowing over the land. I make it to the road and begin to run back toward where I saw Hunter. I have to see him, to explain. I don't care what happens to me as long as I'm with him. I have to tell him that I wanted to stop, that I never would have passed him if I'd had a choice. I've abandoned my car in order to come tell him.

Soon my lungs burn for oxygen, and my running slows. I look behind me, and my fire wings are gone. I can't find Hunter, even though I'm screaming for him! I'm sure I've passed by where I saw him. I've gone back and forth a half dozen times, looking for him, calling his name. I'm soaked through and shivering, my skin rough with goose bumps. My feet hurt. I look down, and then the sharp, dark outline of a hawk overshadows the dusky gray of twilight. I feel a sudden, instantaneous terror—the bird is coming for me. I'm *its prey! Wildly I look up, my arms already raised to protect myself from its attack—*

—and I woke up in my bed, shaking and flooded with adrenaline. I glanced around in panic, but I immediately realized I was in my room. Confused and terrified, I burst into tears, grabbing my pillow and holding it against me. I'd had another nightmare. I braced myself, trying to remember its terrifying details, but found all that remained was a foggy miasma of fear, of panic. But why? What had it been about? I couldn't remember. The memory was slipping away from me. I punched my pillow in frustration, fresh sobs erupting. I muffled them in my pillow, then flopped down on my bed, crying harder. I don't know how long I cried, but eventually I choked to a watery stop and lay there, exhausted.

I had to get to the bottom of this. This was my third night of frightening dreams. What were they about? What was going on with me? Tomorrow after school I would tell Hunter and Alyce and Bethany about them. They were starting to affect my state of mind. I needed help.

And a drink of water. I pushed back the covers, barely noticing that my legs seemed to sting slightly. Then, as I was standing, I glanced down—and froze with horror. My feet and legs were *wet*! They had bits of wet grass clinging to them, as if I had just run across a lawn! And my legs were *scratched* all over, with dozens of tiny scratches, like I had— *Oh, Goddess!* My heart stopped and my blood turned to ice. *Like I had rolled down a thorny embankment.* I had been *outside.* I had been outside while I was *asleep.* Oh, Goddess, what was happening to me?

Shaking, I walked across the room, noting the faint outlines of damp footprints on my sisal rug. My throat was closed with fear, but desperately I cast my senses. I felt nothing out of the ordinary—just my sleeping family. And Dagda? I looked around for my kitten. He always slept with me, often under the covers. I went back and looked on my bed, patting the covers. No Dagda. I made little kissing sounds, calling him. Then I tiptoed out onto the landing and started down the stairs. I saw the barest trace of wet footprints on the stairs and a few pieces of grass. Goddess, Goddess.

Then, at the bottom of the stairs, I saw Dagda's glowing green eyes. He was hunched in front of the front door, his back arched, ears back. He was snarling, showing his teeth. I stared at him, then glanced behind me. There was nothing.

"Dagda, what's wrong?" I asked softly, padding down to get him. He drew back as I reached him, flattening himself against the door, his claws out, looking manic. Low growls came from his throat, along with a sibilant, teakettle hiss.

"Dagda!" I stopped and pulled back my outstretched hand in shock. He was hissing at *me.*

My parents were so surprised to see me the next morning that they stopped talking. Everyone in my family is an early bird, except me. It was a running joke that Mary K. sometimes had to resort to throwing water on my face to get me out of bed in time to get to school.

"Are you okay?" my mom asked, looking at my face. "Did you not sleep well?"

I hadn't further depressed myself by looking in a mirror this morning, but I had a good idea of what I must look like. I moved zombielike to the refrigerator and pawed around inside until I found a Diet Coke. I managed to drink some, hoping the caffeine would help jump-start some brain cells.

"I did not sleep well," I confirmed in an understatement. Automatically I looked around for Dagda and saw him hunched over his bowl, wolfing down kibble. Last night had been so strange—he had never come back into my room.

"Are you sick?" my father asked.

"I don't think so," I said, bracing myself against the kitchen counter. At least not physically, I amended silently. Maybe mentally. I drank some more soda and sat down at my place at the table. "I just haven't been sleeping much."

"Studying," my mom theorized, nodding and clearing her place. "It won't be long till finals. Honey, I'm glad that your schoolwork is getting back up to par, but I don't want you to ruin your health staying up till all hours, studying."

"It's paying off, though," my dad said encouragingly. "You've been bringing home terrific grades, and your mom and I are really pleased."

I gave him a little smile. My grades had nose-dived earlier in the year, in part because of the time and energy I was putting into studying Wicca. My parents had gone ballistic and lowered the boom on me. Now I was studying more, careful to maintain a decent average.

I glanced over at Dagda—he was gone, and as I gazed blankly around the kitchen, I suddenly felt something warm and soft brush against my legs. Cautiously I looked down. My kitten—almost a cat now—was rubbing against me, purring, as he usually did. I tentatively reached down one hand, and he butted his little triangular head against it, demanding ear scratching. Almost weeping with relief—my cat didn't hate me!—I scratched his favorite spots until he flopped limply on the floor in a surfeit of pleasure.

"Morning!" Mary K. said brightly, coming into the kitchen. She looked fabulous, as always, with her clear skin, shining, bouncy hair, and bright brown eyes framed by long lashes.

"Morning, sweetie," Mom answered, and Dad gave Mary K. a fond smile.

My sister pulled a lemon yogurt out of the fridge and sat down at the table. She glanced across at me, taking in my appearance. "Are you sick? What are you doing up?"

"Couldn't sleep," I mumbled, sucking down more caffeine. Several brain cells sprang into action, and it occurred to me that I needed to get dressed for school. Picking up my soda, I headed upstairs to face this new challenge.

I already had Das Boot's motor running when Mary K. climbed in, russet hair swinging forward into her face, Mark Chambers's letter jacket slung around her shoulders. She'd been dating him for a couple of weeks.

"I assume the jacket means things with the beloved Mark are chugging right along?" I asked as I pulled out of our driveway. Mary K.'s face dimpled in a happy smile.

"He's so, so nice," she said, dropping her book bag onto the floor.

"Good. Because if he's a jerk, I'm going to gouge his eyes out."

Mary K. giggled, but her face was shadowed slightly by the meaning and the memory behind my words. "I don't think you'll have to."

What Alisa had said to me on Saturday night suddenly came back to me. "So, have you thought about what to wear to Alisa's dad's wedding?" This had all the subtlety and finesse of a sledgehammer, since I'm notoriously fashion-challenged.

Mary K. looked at me. She wasn't a fool, and I could see she was trying to figure out my angle. "I'm not sure if I'm going to go," she said cautiously.

"Why not? Weddings are fun. And you get cake," I pointed out.

"I don't know," Mary K. said, looking out the car window. "I don't know if Alisa and I have that much in common anymore."

"Because she's half witch," I said, stating the obvious. My sister shrugged.

"Well, I know how you feel about Wicca and the whole blood witch thing," I said. "I know you would feel better if I didn't have anything to do with it and if Alisa didn't have anything to do with it."

Mary K. didn't look at me.

"The thing is," I went on, "no one chooses to be what they are. They just *are*. It's like the color of your eyes or hair or how tall you are. I was born with blood witch genes because my biological parents were blood witches. Alisa is half and half, and there's nothing she can do about it."

My sister sighed.

"In fact," I said, "Alisa herself was really freaked out when she realized she was half witch. I mean, the girl ran away just a few weeks ago because being half witch wasn't something she wanted to sign up for."

Mary K. bit her lip and looked out the window some more.

I had only a few blocks till school. "Do you think Alisa's bitchy?" I asked.

Mary K. turned startled eyes to me. "No."

"Does she lie? Cheat? Steal? Has she moved in on Mark Chambers? Does she say bad stuff about you behind your back?"

"No, of course not," said Mary K. "She's really cool—"

"Exactly. You guys like the same books, movies, clothes. You have similar and incredibly lame senses of humor. You both inexplicably have a crush on Terrence Hagen, the most insipid boy actor ever."

Mary K. was giggling by now. Then her face sobered. I fired my last shot.

"Mary K., you can be friends with whoever you want. If I didn't think that you really cared about Alisa, I would shut up. But you do care about her. And right now Alisa's dad is getting married. She's about to get a new half sibling. She has no real mom. I just think she could use some friends. And between you and me, I think she wouldn't mind it if those friends *didn't* have anything to do with Wicca."

I parked my car in the school lot, the wheels crunching on the small white shells that covered the ground.

"You're right," Mary K. said softly, hauling up her book bag. "I do care about Alisa. I do want to be friends with her."

"Good," I said cheerfully. "And just think, if you're really, really, *really* persistent, you might be able to win her over to Catholicism. Ouch." I rubbed my thigh where Mary K. had just punched me.

"Later, 'gator," she said, just like she used to do when we were little. I smiled at her.

"In a while, crocodile," was my original response.

6

Hunter

I spent most of Tuesday at Practical Magick, helping Alyce sort the books properly. The bookcases in the new room of the store were almost finished. Alyce and I had gone through most of the stock, keeping long, detailed lists of each category. Within each category there were many subcategories, and of course most books had to be cross-referenced. It was engrossing and renewed my interest in reading or rereading some important Wiccan texts, but as with the herb imbuing, it wasn't exactly fulfilling.

I was up on a ladder, calling down titles to Alyce, when I sensed someone coming. The bell over the door jangled in the next moment—Morgan. I glanced at my watch. It was four o'clock already.

"Teatime," I said, starting to climb down the ladder. My hands were filthy with dust, and I wiped them on my jeans. "Hello, my love," I said, meeting Morgan halfway. I held her shoulders lightly and kissed her. "Couldn't stay away from me, I see. I missed you, too."

Her mouth quirked in a nervous smile, then she looked past me to Alyce. "Actually," she said softly, "I need to talk to both of you. Can you spare a couple of minutes?"

"Certainly, dear," said Alyce. She walked to the back of the store and called out to her other employee. "Finn, could you mind the shop for me for a bit?" He nodded and walked to the cash register.

Alyce gestured to the tattered orange curtain that led to the employees' lounge/storage room/lunchroom. Already I was picking up on Morgan's tension, overlain with fatigue, and I wondered what was going on—she hadn't mentioned anything. I rubbed her back as we walked in and sat down. She gave me a strained smile and put her hand on my knee. I tried to read her eyes, but they seemed shuttered, and I went on alert. If something was bothering Morgan, how had I not sensed it before? Or was she hiding something from me?

Within minutes Alyce put three mugs of tea on the table, projecting, as usual, an air of calm, maternal empathy. "What's going on, Morgan? You look very upset."

Morgan nodded and swallowed. I let my arm rest across the back of her chair so she would feel my support. "I've been having . . . dreams," she said. "Nightmares, actually. Scary ones."

I began rubbing her back again with one hand. "These must be somewhat out of the ordinary for you to want to talk to us both about them," I said.

Morgan gave a short, dry laugh. "They're out of the ordinary," she agreed. "They've been going on for three nights now." I put my head to one side, curious, and she turned to me to explain. "I just thought they were ordinary dreams.

Everyone has nightmares sometimes. And nothing that explicitly bad ever happens in them—I'm not seeing murders or anything. They're just really strong, disturbing images. I thought maybe it was stress—finals coming up, that kind of thing. But last night . . ."

She paused to sip her tea, and beneath my hand I felt a fine tremble shake her. "What happened last night?" I asked.

"I had another dream," she said. "I can't even remember most of it. I feel like I keep seeing hawks, dark hawks, in the dreams, but I'm not sure."

I remembered Morgan's response to the hawk we had seen the day of the picnic, and I felt irritated with myself that I hadn't picked up on it. I must be getting thick.

"Last night's dream felt like the worst, but I can't say why," Morgan went on. "All I remember is—I think I was in a car, my car. I wasn't driving, and I had to get out. But it wouldn't stop. I think I jumped out. And when I did, I realized I had bird's wings, but they were made of fire."

Instantly Alyce's eyes met mine. That had to be a symbol for something.

Morgan shook her head, frustrated by not being able to recall more details. "I fell in a ditch, I think. Then I was running on a road, looking for something or someone, and my wings were gone." She shivered again, though it was warm in the room, and hunched her shoulders as if to protect herself. "But that's not the worst part," she said in a small voice. "The worst part is that when I woke up, my legs and feet were wet. And there were little bits of dried grass stuck to me."

"Oh, Morgan." My muscles tensed. Goddess. This was incredibly serious.

"And I had these," Morgan said, pulling up the sleeve of her shirt. Her arm was crisscrossed with many fine scratches. "My legs are scratched, too." She sounded afraid but was trying not to show it. "So I was *sleepwalking*. I went downstairs and saw wet footprints all the way to the front door. And Dagda—" Her voice broke off, and she gripped her mug in both hands. "I saw Dagda and went to him, and he hunched up like a Halloween kitty and *hissed* at me. Like I scared him." Her voice wavered. She was obviously fighting back tears. I scooted my chair closer to her and tried to wrap my arm around her protectively.

Alyce's kind, round face showed some of the concern I was feeling, though she still looked calm.

"Have you ever sleepwalked before?" I asked.

Morgan shook her head. "Never."

"The other two nights you had these dreams . . . do you think you were sleepwalking then?"

Morgan frowned, trying to remember. She shook her head, and her hair brushed back and forth against my arm. "Not that I know of."

Alyce sat back, looking at Morgan thoughtfully. "Goodness," she said. "You must feel very frightened, dear."

Morgan nodded, not looking at her. Alyce reached out and covered Morgan's hand with her own. "I don't blame you. I would be upset, too. What else do you remember about the dreams? Any kind of detail, anything at all. What about the first dream?"

Morgan sighed. "I remember waking up and knowing I'd had a bad dream and that I was kind of upset, but I just put it out of my mind. All I could remember about it was my feet hurting."

I smiled at her in encouragement.

"The next dream I remember better," Morgan said, "because I was determined not to repeat it again last night. I remember running through huge halls, like in a mansion. I kept getting lost. I looked through the window to get my bearings, and outside there were more walls, floating there. They were covered with writing, but I don't remember any of it. I remember running past the windows, and when I passed them, their curtains caught on fire. And there was a hawk, I think." Her forehead wrinkled as she tried to remember anything else. Then she shook her head. "That's all I remember."

"Was there a fire in the first dream?" I asked, looking for common threads.

"I don't remember. I don't think so. But maybe? Maybe I smelled smoke?" Morgan looked frustrated and confused.

"Okay," said Alyce, patting her hand reassuringly. "Let's look at what we have. You said that hawks were a part of your dreams. Do you remember what they were doing, how they looked?"

Morgan slowly shook her head. "I don't remember. I just *feel* like they've been in all of my dreams."

"All right," said Alyce. "Usually dreaming about birds symbolizes freedom or happiness."

"Yes, but she's dreaming about raptors, birds of prey," I pointed out. "That could indicate greed or a power struggle. Having a dark-feathered hawk to me seems more ominous: sensing danger or threat." I didn't know all that much about dream interpretation. I had learned just enough to pass my initiation, but I remembered a few of the common symbols.

"What about me having wings with flames on them?" Morgan asked.

Alyce shot me a hesitant glance.

"Well, fire usually symbolizes purification, cleansing," I said.

"Or sometimes metamorphosis, something changing from one form to another," Alyce added. "But you also have personal connections to it."

Morgan nodded solemnly. She had shown a special affinity for fire ever since she'd first learned she was a blood witch. She was one of the few blood witches I'd ever known who could successfully scry with fire. There was also family history with fire. Apparently her birth mother, Maeve Riordan, had also shown an affinity for it. Until she'd been burned to death.

"There's something else," Alyce said, looking thoughtful. "A bird with wings of fire . . . It's ringing a bell, but I can't quite place my finger on it. I feel like I've heard of that somewhere before." She thought for another few moments, then shook her head briskly. "Well, we'll need to do research on that one and on the curtains catching fire. Now, the car. Cars often represent the path you're taking through life, the path you're taking to achieve goals."

I frowned, trying to recall old lessons. "And being a passenger symbolizes someone having control over you, dictating your path."

"Walls can represent either safety or confinement. The halls you ran down were also a life path. The symbols you couldn't understand represented your literal confusion about something, that there's something going on you don't understand." Alyce leaned forward, thinking.

"I'm hearing a lot about life paths, sensed danger, and also confusion, hidden stuff," I said uncomfortably. "These symbols seem to keep repeating themselves."

"Yes," Alyce agreed. She looked at Morgan. "You need to do some deep thinking, dear. Some meditation might help make some of this clear. To me it feels like there's something hanging over your head, symbolically if not literally. The fact that these dreams are so strong, strong enough to make you actually sleepwalk, means we must take them very seriously. Your psyche is sending you a powerful message. It's important that we figure out what it is."

Morgan looked troubled. "There's something else that I just thought of," she said. "The walls with the writing on them, the symbols and runes—they remind me of Cal's *seòmar*—his secret room where he worked all that dark magick."

And where he had tried to kill her. My stomach knotted, and fury boiled up in me like lava. My half brother, Cal, was dead, yet it seemed Morgan would never be free of his influence, his corruption. He'd nearly seduced her, manipulated her, and tried to steal her power. For a minute I was so angry, my teeth clenched so tightly, that I couldn't speak. Then I spit out the obvious. "But Cal is dead."

"I know," Morgan said in frustration. "I don't understand any of it. All I know is that it's making me crazy, and now I'm actually *sleepwalking*. That's just too much for me to deal with." She put her elbows on the table and dropped her face into her hands.

"We have to sort this out quickly," I said to Alyce, surprising myself with the harshness of my voice. "Morgan's obviously in danger. We have to figure out where the threat is coming from and eliminate it."

"I agree," Alyce said, regarding me calmly. "But the 'threat' could be coming from Morgan herself. Her psyche could simply be using strong means to get a message across. The sooner we figure out that message, the sooner it can stop trying to make an impression on her."

"I don't believe that," I said, looking at Alyce evenly. "I know Morgan. I don't think her psyche would cause her to sleepwalk in the middle of the night to get its point across. I believe these dreams are magickal."

"I hate this," Morgan muttered, shaking her head. I stroked her hair down her back, smoothing the heavy strands.

"I know," Alyce said, patting Morgan's hand again. "I don't blame you. It's hard to sort out. But one thing is clear: These dreams might be serious, and we need to take action."

"On the chance that these dreams could be influenced or caused by an outside source, I'm going to research how one would do that," I said. "Maybe I can suss out some examples of cases where it was found that outside forces were influencing a person's dreams. And perhaps I'll talk to my father about otherworld influences acting in this world."

Like dead people, coming back to terrorize Morgan. Like Cal. Or maybe a living person, someone from Amyranth, someone who was possibly doing Ciaran's bidding. I nodded at Alyce, already considering how to go about it.

"Morgan, I'd like you to do some self-examination," Alyce said. "Meditate, think, work revealing spells—anything you can think of that might help explain what these dreams are about."

"You might want to do this when you feel safe, like when your parents are home or with me," I suggested. "Any other details that come to you, any snatches of memory or insights or fragments, write down. Keep a record of everything."

"Okay," Morgan said, sounding glum.

"As for myself, I'll do more research into dream symbolism," Alyce said.

"I'm curious about what the fire-winged hawk might mean," I said, and she agreed.

"Also," Alyce said, "I'll make you a tisane today—a simple drink that will help you sleep and prevent you from dreaming further until we can get a handle on what's going on."

"That would be great," Morgan said in relief. "I'm afraid to go back to sleep after all of this."

Alyce clucked sympathetically, then got up and filled the copper teakettle with fresh water. "I'll fix you something that will help, at least for the next night or two. Just be sure to drink it at least ten hours before you have to get up the next day. If you have to get up at seven-thirty for school, drink it no later than nine-thirty the night before. Or else you'll be slow and sleepy at school."

"We don't want *that*," Morgan said dryly, and I laughed, despite my concern. A morning person, she wasn't.

"All right, then," Alyce said, bustling about, opening cupboards and taking out different herbs and oils. She put valerian, kava kava, and ginseng on the counter. "Morgan, why don't you and Hunter visit while I get this ready? It should take me about half an hour, forty minutes."

"Good idea," I said, standing and tugging on Morgan's hand. She got up.

"Thanks, Alyce," she said.

Alyce smiled at her. "My pleasure. We're both here for you—I'm really glad you came to us. You don't have to fight these battles alone. Not anymore."

Morgan smiled a bit, then we left the back room and headed

to the new half of the store. Inside my little work area I closed the door and pulled Morgan onto my lap. She rested her head against my shoulder, and I felt her comfortable weight settle closer. I threw a quick "delay" spell at the door. It wouldn't actually keep anyone out, but it would slow them down for a few seconds.

"Morgan, I wish you had told me," I murmured against her hair.

"I thought they were just ordinary dreams," she said. "But this morning when I realized I'd been *outside*—" Her fear was plain in her voice, and I held her closer.

"We'll take care of it," I promised her. "We'll figure it out, and you'll be fine again. At least tonight you know you're going to sleep really well."

"Mmm-hmm," she said.

For long minutes I held her on my lap, stroking her hair and gradually feeling the tension in her slender body uncoil. She relaxed so completely against me that I almost thought she had fallen asleep.

"Hunter?" she said.

"Hmm?"

"I'm tired of being afraid," she said. Her voice was very calm, almost matter-of-fact, but it struck a chord deep within me. Ever since she had realized she was a blood witch, her life had been a cascade of incredible highs and wretched lows. We both felt ready to have some smooth sailing for a while.

"I know, my love," I said, kissing her temple.

"I wish I could get out of here."

I'd never heard her say anything like that before. "You mean, like come to England with me this summer?"

I felt her smile. "I wish. No, I just feel like I need to get out of here for a while. Like I keep getting layers of bad emotions. All through the autumn and winter. Now through the spring. I need to go someplace else and start over. At least for a while."

"Let's think about it," I said. "Let's try to come up with a way to make that happen for you."

"Okay." She stifled a yawn.

It wasn't long before we felt Alyce approaching, and Morgan stood up to lean against my worktable. I heard Alyce reach for the doorknob a couple of times, apparently missing it, and I wondered if she sensed the delay spell. If she did, she didn't make any mention of it.

"Here you go," she said, coming into the room. She held out a small brown bottle with a screw-on lid and put it into a Practical Magick shopping bag. "Drink half of it tonight and save half for tomorrow. Don't mix it with anything else, and don't drink or eat anything else for two hours before or after you drink it."

"Okay," said Morgan, taking the bag. "And this will really keep me from sleepwalking?"

"It will," Alyce promised.

"Thanks," Morgan said. "Thanks so much. You don't know how much I've been dreading going back to sleep."

"Take care, and we'll talk tomorrow." Alyce gave Morgan one last smile and headed back to the shop.

"Do you think you'll be all right tonight?" I asked.

Morgan nodded. Her beautiful eyes were dark with worry and fatigue. "I'll be okay."

7

Morgan

Alyce's tisane didn't taste quite as bad as I thought it would. At nine that night I managed to get it down by holding my nose and swallowing it in two gulps.

Now it was ten, and I was distinctly woozy. I got off my mom's bed—we'd been watching her favorite cop show together—and told everyone good night. I got into a big T-shirt and brushed my teeth and fell into bed. Almost immediately, using his superkitty senses, Dagda knew it was bedtime and came trotting through the bathroom. Sleepily I patted the bed and he leaped up, making no sound and hardly any vibration.

With Dagda purring hard next to me, I went through some guided relaxation exercises, affirming that I felt safe, that I would sleep well, that everything was fine, that my subconscious would reveal anything I needed to know. I pictured myself sleeping like a log until morning. I pictured myself safe and surrounded by protective white light. I pictured all my worries and fears floating away from me like helium balloons.

I got sleepier and sleepier until I realized I wasn't even thinking straight. Then I let go of the day and embraced sleep.

Why are you trying to avoid me? The words clawed their way into my brain as I struggled to wake up. Dimly I knew I was floating upward toward consciousness and felt a tinge of panic, as if I shouldn't be leaving this soon. *Why are you trying to avoid me? Come join me.* The words were white slashes against the dark backdrop of my sleep.

Suddenly, just as I was beginning to sense the sheet gripped in my hands, an image flashed: a dark-feathered hawk, streaking away. It was being chased by another hawk, rust colored and cruel eyed, who seemed terrible and strong and whose powerful wings were edged with flames.

I looked down, as if I were one of the hawks, and saw the ground far beneath me, grids of gold and green. With frighteningly clear hawk sight I saw a lone person standing in a field of wheat. Like a laser, my eyes zoomed in on the figure, and as I swooped closer, the person looked up and smiled.

At that moment I woke up and sat bolt upright in bed, my heart racing, clutching the sheet to my chest with fingers like claws.

It had been Cal.

"Will you *stop?*"

Robbie quit drumming his fingers on the lunch table and looked at me in hurt surprise. My heart sank. I was being a total bitch.

"I'm sorry," I said stiffly. "I'm having a bad day."

Understatement of the year. Ever since I had seen Cal in

my dream last night, I'd felt like my whole world had shifted. Cal is dead. Cal is dead. That was what I'd been telling myself for the past five months. But now he was trying to contact me when I was most vulnerable—while I slept. What did he *want*? Where, who, or what was he? I couldn't make sense of any of it. I was frightened, confused, horrified—and a small, terrible part of me was flattered. Maybe even happy. Cal had done horrible things, but he'd loved me, in his own twisted way. I loved Hunter now, but the thought that Cal might be trying to contact me from the *dead* was a sick kind of ego boost.

"You've been kind of off all week," Bree said, with typical best-friend frankness. "Are you and Hunter okay?"

I pushed my school lunch of clumpy mac and cheese away and grimaced. "Hunter's fine. School's fine. Folks are fine."

"Sister's fiiiiine," sang Mary K., dipping quickly to get that in as she passed by on her way to the Mary K. fan club table.

Bree giggled, watching Mary K. weave through the cafeteria, brown lunch bag swinging at her side. "So what isn't fine?" she asked, turning back to me.

I sighed heavily. How to put this? "I think my dead ex-boyfriend's spirit is trying to terrorize or even physically hurt me"? Why didn't I just call Jerry Springer *now*? "I've been having bad dreams," I said inadequately. "They've been keeping me up."

Bree and Robbie both looked unimpressed. I saw them glance quickly at each other and make a decision: Let's just walk on eggshells until she chills out.

As soon as I had cleared my tray, I called Hunter and asked him to pick me up after school.

* * *

Seeing a six-foot-plus length of blond, handsome witch leaning against his car and grinning did a lot to calm me down.

"Hi," I said, knowing I sounded pathetic. Hunter folded me in his arms, and I let my head sink against his chest. My whole life, I had been strong and self-sufficient. I'd always thought of those as good qualities. Now I was experimenting with relying on someone else. So far, it was going pretty well.

"I'm glad you called," Hunter said. "I was going to send you a message. I have to go and collect Sky at the airport. Can you go with me?"

"I think so. Let me call my mom." I borrowed Hunter's cell phone and dialed my mom's office number. She said it was okay. With relief I made sure that Mary K. got a ride home, then I left Das Boot all by its lonesome in the parking lot and climbed into Hunter's anonymous green Honda.

"I'm so glad to see you," I said, turning to him and scooting as close as I could.

He leaned over and gave me a lingering kiss, then started the engine. "How did it go last night? I wanted to call you this morning to see but didn't know if it would be a good idea."

"I had a dream," I said, looking out the window.

"No," he said, frowning. "Even after taking Alyce's potion?"

I nodded. "I followed all her directions. I think for the most part, I didn't dream that much. But right before dawn I heard a voice."

Hunter looked at me, then pulled onto the entrance to the highway. "What did it say?"

"It said, 'Why are you trying to avoid me?'" I repeated,

trying not to let my remembered fear overcome me. "Twice."

"Goddess," Hunter said. He rubbed his chin with one hand, the way he did when he was thinking something through. "That isn't good."

"No, I didn't think so," I said wryly. "And I saw hawks again. Just for a second, but they were there. A dark hawk being chased by a fire-winged hawk. Then it looked like I was a hawk, flying overhead. I looked down and saw someone standing in a field."

"And?"

I couldn't help shuddering. "And it was Cal."

The car gave a sudden swerve, and I grabbed my door handle.

"Sorry," said Hunter. "I'm sorry, Morgan. So you saw Cal in your dream?" He was trying to sound casual, but I knew him, and his voice was tight. He had hated Cal to the very bone and still got tense at the mention of his name.

"Yes." I shook my head. "That's when I woke up. Maybe Alyce's drink wore off right before I was going to wake up, and that's why I suddenly had all these dream images."

"Maybe," said Hunter, sounding grim. "Well, we'll find out more tonight. I've arranged for us to meet with Alyce and Bethany tonight, at Bethany's apartment. Is eight o'clock okay?"

"Yeah, no problem. Did you tell Bethany what's going on?"

"Alyce did, and Bethany's concerned, like we all are."

I leaned my head against Hunter's shoulder, feeling the warmth of his skin through his thin jacket. I couldn't wait till it got really warm and Hunter would be wearing T-shirts and shorts. Thinking about that cheered me up a little.

"How did Sky sound when she called?" I asked.

"Ready to come home," Hunter said, and grinned.

We turned into the airport and Hunter pulled into the pickup spot he had arranged with Sky. We had been waiting only a few minutes when we spotted Sky's white-blond hair bobbing through the crowd. Soon her thin, black-clad body appeared, tugging a large green suitcase on wheels behind her. She spotted Hunter and waved. They were first cousins, but more important, they had grown up together, living like brother and sister since Hunter was eight.

"Sky! Over here!" Hunter called, and Sky's fine-boned face split into a grin.

"I'm back," she said, and then she and Hunter were hugging, and he lifted her off her feet. "Goddess, what did you do to your hair?" she said critically when they pulled apart. Since his hair looked exactly the same as it always had, I knew she was just teasing him.

"What?" said Hunter, running his hand over his short blond spikes. "What's wrong with it?"

Sky caught my eye and smirked, and I laughed. She swung her suitcase into the trunk with effort. "Hallo, Morgan," she said, somewhat formally but with a nod.

"Welcome back," I said, getting in the car next to Hunter. Sky got in the back. I half turned in my seat so I could see both of them at once.

"I'm looking forward to seeing Uncle Daniel," Sky said, watching Hunter carefully. "How's he been?"

"He's getting better, I think," said Hunter. "Healthier. He's giving talks about spellcrafting at covens around the area. He's not thrilled by my quitting the council."

"Have you heard from Kennet since you called to quit?"

"No."

Seeming to want to change the subject, Sky said, "Oh! I brought you some small tokens of my affection." She rummaged in her backpack and pulled out various paper and plastic bags. Hunter sat up, interested, and I hoped he was paying attention to the road.

"A jar of Marmite," Sky said, holding up a smallish brown jar.

"Yes!" Hunter said enthusiastically. I'd never heard of Marmite and wondered if it was a jam or something.

"Some PG Tips tea, tea of peers," Sky continued, tossing a large yellow box into the front seat.

"Bless you," Hunter murmured.

"A package of actual crumpets, only slightly mashed."

"Crumpets," Hunter repeated, sounding blissful.

"McVitie's." Sky dropped a couple of round cookie packages over my shoulder. From the picture on the front, they looked like round graham crackers.

"And for Morgan, a lovely new tea towel featuring the family tree of Her Royal Majesty." She tossed a folded rectangle of linen into my lap.

Hunter cackled. "Too brilliant."

"Oh," I said, surprised. "Thank you. This was really nice of you." I shook it out and grinned. "This is great."

"Every home needs one." Sky sat back against her seat. "So, any news?"

"Um, Alisa's coming to terms with being half witch."

"Good. It might be rough for a while," said Sky.

"Dagda caught a vole in the yard." I was trying to think of

more interesting things that didn't have to do with my nightmares but was running short.

"Stout lad," Sky approved. "And what news of your half brother?"

My jaw almost dropped. Killian was the only one of my three half siblings I had met, and I had mixed feelings about him. On the one hand, he was charming, funny, generous, and generally well meaning. On the other, he was irreverent, thoughtless, undependable, and somewhat amoral. One night Sky had gotten drunk and had ended up in a compromising position with him in his room. Raven and I had found them. Sky and Raven had just broken up. A nasty scene had ensued.

"He's doing fine. You know Killian," I said cautiously.

Sky looked nonchalantly out her window. I wondered if she'd wanted to ask about Raven but couldn't, so she'd asked about Killian instead. Hmmm.

"Morgan, I'm going to drop you at your car before I take Sky home," Hunter said, and with surprise I noticed we had already turned onto the Widow's Vale exit.

"Okay."

At school Das Boot was the only car left in the lot. Hunter walked me over to it. "I'll see you in about an hour and a half," he said softly, leaning down to kiss me.

"At Bethany's." Just thinking about it made me feel better.

I climbed into Das Boot and started it, watching while Sky got into the front seat. I couldn't help being a little jealous of Sky. She got to live with Hunter, see him all the time. It was what *I* wanted. Hunter waited till I had started my car and headed off before he went in his own direction.

* * *

At ten after eight I hurried up the stairs at the front entrance to Bethany's apartment house. It was dark, and the streetlight shone amber on the building. A movement caught my eye, and I turned to see a large dark shadow taking off into the air. I followed its silhouette, but the streetlight shone right in my eyes, making it hard to see.

"Damn crows. They're everywhere," an older man said, coming up the steps after me. He gave me a casual smile and went past, holding the door for me.

Maybe it *had* just been a crow. Maybe. I followed him in and hustled up to Bethany's apartment.

"Morgan!" Bethany said warmly, opening the door to my knock. Her dark brown eyes shone with concern, and her short black hair was arranged haphazardly in a pixie style. "How are you? Come in, come in." Rubbing my back, she followed me into her smallish living room, where Hunter and Alyce were already waiting.

"Hi. Sorry I'm late," I said, taking off my jacket and dropping it on the floor next to a chair. I suddenly felt a little self-conscious—everyone was here because of *my* problems. I sat down and tucked my hands under my legs so they wouldn't clench nervously. These three people cared about me. They had all helped me before, and I had helped them. We were friends. I could trust them.

"I told Alyce and Bethany about last night's dream," Hunter said.

"It sounds . . . very disconcerting," Bethany said. That was an understatement. She arranged herself comfortably on the overstuffed couch.

"I did some research," she said, "after Alyce told me about this last night. But first, I know you've told Hunter and

Alyce all you remember, but I'd like to hear it again for myself, if you don't mind."

"Okay," I said. Once again I related what I could remember of the dreams I'd had but couldn't come up with any new details. Bethany jotted a few notes as I spoke, and I was aware that Hunter and Alyce were listening attentively.

"So that's it," I concluded. "But last night was the first one where I felt like I saw someone who might have something to do with the dreams."

Bethany nodded. "Alyce, do you still feel that these dreams might be coming from Morgan's subconscious? That it's trying to send her a message?"

"Not as much, not after last night's dream," Alyce admitted. "The voice asking about being avoided, actually seeing Cal. I have to say, it now sounds like these dreams are coming *to* Morgan, not coming *from* Morgan."

"Oh, Goddess," I said, feeling my stomach cave in. "It was bad enough when I thought I had something inside *me* to work out. But now I'm being attacked?" My voice sounded whiny, but I couldn't help it. I felt so afraid and frustrated and angry that it was all I could do not to jump up and start screaming.

"Assuming that it's Cal," Hunter said, "it isn't clear how he's doing this." I could see a vein in his neck standing out and knew he was controlling his anger only with difficulty. "The few times I've had any contact with the otherworld, it's been with the anam of a very powerful person. My research turned up much the same information. I would have thought Cal's powers weren't strong enough."

"What's an anam?" I asked.

"A . . . soul," Alyce said. "A spirit, an essence. The *you* that remains after your body is gone. And yes, I agree that one must be very strong to do this. Of course I didn't know him well at all."

"What's even more important is *why* he would be doing this," Bethany said. "What does he want? What's his aim?"

"Besides turning me into a screaming lunatic," I said bitterly.

"To get control of Morgan, obviously," Hunter said. "It's what he always wanted."

"But what good would I be now?" I asked. "He's gone, Selene's gone. He sacrificed himself to save me. What would he want from me now?"

Hunter looked down at his feet. I knew he still hated Cal. He'd never believed that Cal had tried to save me. I reached out and took his hand.

"I don't know, dear," Alyce said. "We need to find out. In the meantime let's compare notes and research. Maybe some of it will start to fall into place."

"I think we can't rule out that it's someone else, perhaps working through or with Cal's anam," Bethany said thoughtfully. "Right now he's our main suspect, but it would be foolish to settle on him as the answer until we know for sure."

"I can't believe this." I shook my head. Why? Why was he doing this to me? "I feel so powerless. For him—or whoever—to do this while I'm sleeping, when I'm totally helpless and at his mercy . . . I can't stand it."

"You're not totally helpless, my dear," said Alyce. "We need to talk about interactive dreaming, guided dreaming."

"Hold on," Hunter said. His voice sounded hoarse.

I looked over at him and saw a sick look on his face. He turned to me.

"That night in Selene's library—we saw Cal and Selene die. But what happened then? We got Mary K. and hustled out of there—I wanted to make sure you were both safe."

"Uh-huh," I said, hating to remember that horrible night. "What are you getting at?"

"What happened to their bodies?" Hunter asked, and I felt the blood drain from my face.

I forced my memory back, back to seeing Cal crumple under Selene's dark power, the bolt of evil meant to kill me that he had taken instead. I remembered holding Selene in a sort of magickal crystal cage. And then she had died. They had both been lying motionless on the library floor. We had left, and outside, Sky was just arriving with some council members. They had streamed into the house, and I hadn't looked back.

My gaze met Hunter's, and I felt hollow. "I don't know," I said. "We left them there. They were dead."

Hunter stood and headed for Bethany's phone. Quickly he punched in a long number, then waited, pacing in tight circles.

"Kennet?" he said after a moment. "Yes—sorry. I know it's late. I wouldn't have woken you, but this is important. Listen, I must know—what did the council do with the bodies of Cal Blaire and Selene Belltower?"

I watched him, feeling clouded by sorrow and memory.

"No, I understand, but it's important, I promise," Hunter said. He listened silently, his face becoming more and more set.

"Kennet—I appreciate that. I know I'm no longer on the council, and I know there are things that don't need to be broadcast. But this is me, and I'm asking you, as a friend. Please, can you just tell me what happened to their bodies?"

He listened for a while more, then seemed to lose his patience. "Kennet, please. Right now I don't care about the council or its protocols or what anyone is authorized to say. I need some answers—it's a matter of life and death."

His face was grim and tense. I knew Kennet had been his mentor and his friend.

"You're quite sure? Did you see it? You saw this yourself?" His head tilted to one side, and it occurred to me that he was probably analyzing Kennet's voice to determine whether he was telling the truth.

"Yes, all right. I understand. Yes, I know. Thank you, Kennet. I appreciate it. You won't regret telling me. Good-bye, then." Abruptly he hung up, then wiped his forehead, pushing his short hair up as he did. He came back and sat down next to me, taking one of my hands in his. I waited, staring into his eyes.

"Cal and Selene's bodies were taken back to England, where they were cremated. Their urns were interred in a small family mausoleum near Selene's birthplace. Kennet swears he actually saw the bodies cremated. I believe he was telling the truth, or at least the truth as he knows it."

I felt a sense of relief. "I guess it can't be them, then."

"Not necessarily," said Alyce gently. "This tells us that neither Cal nor Selene had a chance to go back into their own bodies. But it doesn't mean their anams were destroyed—just their physical beings."

"But how could they survive this long?" I asked. "How could they get to me now?"

"I don't know," Alyce admitted. "That's one of the questions we need to answer."

"Let's talk about what actions we can take now," said Bethany firmly, and for the next hour she and Alyce coached me in both interactive and guided dreaming. Before I went to sleep, I could deliberately decide to take part in my dreams, to be able to take action in them. Once there I could guide my dreams the way I wanted them to go; for example, I could *find* a door, *stop* my car, be unafraid of anything I might see or hear.

"I know this will help. I just wish I didn't have to do any of this," I said.

"I understand," said Bethany. "But for tonight we'll try to give you a reprieve. I've created a very strong sleeping draught that should really knock you out, no dreams. If you do somehow dream, use the exercises we've gone over. But I'm confident that you'll wake up tomorrow feeling better, safer. And by tomorrow evening we hope to have more solid information about how dreams can be influenced either in the real world or from the netherworld."

"Thanks," I said. "I really appreciate you all helping me like this."

"Of course," Bethany said, and smiled.

I was supposed to be home by ten, so I got my jacket, took Bethany's little bottle, and said good-bye. Hunter wanted to walk me out, and I wasn't about to discourage him.

Outside, my car glowed under the streetlight, heavy and familiar and safe. I opened the door and leaned against it for a minute.

"I'm sorry, Morgan," said Hunter, brushing my hair back. "We'll fix this somehow, I promise."

"Thanks," I said. "I just feel . . . like I'll be paying for my mistakes for the rest of my life." The mistake of trusting Cal, of loving him.

"You won't," said Hunter, and he sounded so sure that I wanted to believe him. "Listen, do you want me to stay outside your house tonight? Just in case?"

I thought about it. "No," I decided. "The only time I sleepwalked was before any of you were helping me. I feel okay about the interactive dreaming stuff. Plus I have Bethany's magick potion." I held up the small purple bottle.

"All right," said Hunter, sounding reluctant. "But call me if you need anything."

"I will." We kissed and hugged, not wanting to let go.

Then I got in my car and started the engine. Hunter got smaller and smaller in my rearview mirror until I turned the corner at the next block.

8

Hunter

I got home from Bethany's by ten-fifteen and found Sky making a pot of tea.

"I knew there was a reason that I missed you," I said, and she swatted me with a tea towel. "Put out a mug for me, will you? Is Da out? Did you two talk much?"

She nodded, putting my mug on the table.

I love Sky, I respect Sky, and I know who Sky is underneath. She can be funny and warm and thoughtful. Though sometimes I worry that someone who doesn't know her like I do might be put off by how self-contained she is.

"He's something, your da," she said, sitting down with her mug of tea. "He went out for an hour. Should be back soon. He seems quite different from the way you described him when you first saw him."

"He's night-and-day different," I assured her. "He's going to seem like my old da any day now."

Sky made a face at my cheekiness and took a sip of tea.

"How's your corner working out?" I asked. One thing

none of us had thought of was that our house had only two bedrooms. Da had immediately offered to give up his, which had once been Sky's, but she wouldn't let him. I had done the chivalrous thing and offered my room, too. But I had to admit to myself that I was relieved when she didn't take me up on it. Not when I still had hopes of getting Morgan in there someday alone. So we had rigged up a makeshift curtain across a small alcove that might have once been a pantry, off the dining room. There was just enough space for a single futon, small table, and reading lamp. Oddly, it seemed to suit Sky's somewhat spartan needs.

"Corner's fine," she said. "Very cozy. In fact, I'm heading there now. Jet lag is knocking me on my back." She stood up and automatically carried her mug to the sink.

"Good to have you back," I said, catching her hand as she went past. She gave mine a squeeze, then headed into the dining room.

Around eleven my father came home. I was waiting in the kitchen and had a mug of tea ready for him. He looked grateful, if somewhat surprised, at my thoughtfulness. He filled me in on his latest speaking dates, and I decided to let him in on Morgan's dreams. I felt a bit odd talking to him about it. Cal had been Da's son, just as much as I was. It wasn't hard for me to hate a half brother I had hardly known, but I knew that Da had much more conflicted feelings. For one thing, I knew he blamed himself for leaving Cal, his infant son, with Selene, in order to be able to marry my own mother, Fiona. He would always question whether Cal would have practiced dark magick if he'd grown up with us, in our family. We'd never know. I deliberately kept my tone as neutral as I could, but I saw a familiar weight bow his shoulders.

"That sounds bad," he said quietly, stroking his chin. "Do what you can, lad."

"What do you think of the possibility of Cal's anam coming back this way?"

"It would be extremely unusual," he said. "Despite all the fairy tales, it's incredibly difficult and rare for someone to come back from the netherworld—at least, not without a lot of help." His face was taut, and by unspoken agreement we didn't discuss how he had once supplied that help to others. "And I didn't know Cal, mind, but I wouldn't have thought he was strong enough."

"Right, that's what we think, too. And there's something else," I said, moving on quickly. I felt glad I had someone I could trust to talk about Patrice Pearson with. My father, for all his parental idiosyncrasies, could actually be very helpful at sorting out what was happening with the Willowbrook coven. I knew he could be trusted, and he was experienced in the ways of dark magick. I told him everything that Celia Evans and Robin Goodacre had told me, along with my own impressions of them. He listened attentively, giving a low whistle when I described how drained the women felt after a circle and how they sometimes felt they couldn't remember the entire evening.

"Sounds like a job for a Seeker," he said meaningfully, but I shook my head.

"I think I can do more not being a Seeker. Anyhow, I need to start investigating. I was wondering if you felt up to some spying and scrying tonight."

"Me?"

"Yes. I'm not sure how strong Patrice is—I could use someone else's powers, and then, you might also see things I would miss."

"Are you referring to breaking and entering?"

"Nooo. Strictly outside work."

He nodded, considering, then grinned. "Let me get my jacket."

Celia had given me Patrice's address, and we located it without much trouble. Forty minutes after leaving my place I drove past her house, which turned out to be a large, well-maintained Victorian in a historic section of Thornton. I parked around the corner, then made sure my mobile was on and set to vibrate. I had faith that Bethany's potion would work, but I wanted to be available if Morgan needed me.

Da and I were dressed in dark clothes, and we said a few see-me-not spells on our way to Patrice's house. We also put up some basic blocking spells: Patrice might feel the presence of other blood witches, but before she could investigate, she would be distracted by something. It was almost midnight; she was probably asleep. But just in case, we wanted to be smart.

It was a quiet, moonless night, and I was thankful for magesight as I picked my way unerringly through her neighbors' backyards. The air was still and quite chilly, but the late spring scent of newly opened flowers drifted toward me, and I inhaled appreciatively. From the very back of her property we looked up at her house. One or two windows had a slight glow to them, as if there were night-lights on. That seemed odd—night-lights were one thing you didn't often find in a witch's house. Then I remembered her ill, uninitiated son and figured he must be the reason.

Neither Da nor I sensed any kind of activity from the house, so we wove our way silently to her large backyard garden. It was a real witch's garden, I saw, with neat beds, raked paths, and green everywhere. I read the small copper signs, seeing the familiar plants: burdock, beetroot, rosemary, yarrow, thistle, goldenseal, mullein, nettle, skullcap. Herbs for dyeing, herbs for tinctures, herbs for healing, soothing, cleansing. Very appropriate.

Then I saw the neat row of foxglove at the back of one bed. Then I looked around more and noticed Da doing the same. Wordlessly he pointed to a plant. Even in the dark I identified it as a young castor bean plant. By autumn it could be up to ten feet tall, with seedpods full of attractive seeds that people make necklaces out of. Hopefully no one would decide to chew on their necklace because it would likely kill them. I began walking slowly around the beds, becoming concerned, but didn't see anything else out of the ordinary.

I signaled to my father, and we crept across the yard to sit beneath a huge oak tree.

"Interesting," he said in a barely audible tone.

"Very."

"Of course, a great many plants are poisonous, and people still have them," I said. "Because they're pretty or useful in a nonedible way. Laurels, rhododendrons, oleander, yew. They're everywhere."

"But castor bean? Nightshade?" said Da skeptically.

"No. It doesn't look good." Deep in the shadows here, I pulled out my scrying stone, a large, flat piece of obsidian that

Da had left me when I was eight. He gave a small nod of recognition. Together we placed our fingertips around the very edge of the stone, and I said the little scrying rhyme Sky and I had made up so many years ago. It had always served me well and could be adapted for any number of situations.

Stone of jet, hue of night
Help us as we join our sight
Let us scry the one we seek
She whose name we now will speak.
Patrice Pearson.

I traced the rune of Sigel over the stone to help us achieve clarity. Then I concentrated on my heartbeat slowing down, my breathing becoming more shallow, my focus and gaze centering on the stone before me. Almost immediately a very clear image of a dark-haired woman came to me. She was in a darkened room and was lifting something in the air. I didn't realize what it was at first, but then I recognized it as an IV bag. Patrice hooked it onto some sort of metal frame. In the next instant she looked up, as if she had just felt us scrying for her. She frowned.

"Here we go," said Da, and we leaped to our feet. Within seconds the back door of Patrice's house had opened, and we heard the furious barks and snarls of a dog tearing toward us in the dark.

"Run!" I said needlessly—Da was already outpacing me by a yard. We fairly flew through the neighbors' yards, pounded down the sidewalk, and scrabbled at the door handles of my car.

As soon as he slammed the car door shut, we heard a

heavy thunk against the metal: the dog hitting the car. Outraged barks were barely muted by the closed windows.

"Goddess," Da breathed, pushing his hair off his face. "Fierce bugger."

I started the engine, planning to do a quick U-turn so I wouldn't have to pass Patrice's house. My father peered through the windows.

"What is it?" I panted, feeling adrenaline pulsing through my veins. I'd been bitten by a dog before, as a Seeker, and it had been incredibly painful. "A rottweiler? Mastiff?"

My father started chuckling—an unusual sound, coming from him. It sounded like rusty nails being shaken in a can. "It's a dachshund," he said, really starting to laugh. "It's a long-haired dachshund. Look, you can see him when he jumps up to the window."

I looked across and saw a small, elegant brown head lift into my sight for a moment, then sink down again. A moment's pause and then once more his little face appeared, teeth bared viciously, horrible-sounding snarls coming from his throat. Then he sank down, no doubt already mustering the strength for another determined leap.

I snorted with laughter, almost choking, as I pulled slowly and carefully away from the curb. "Oh, Goddess, Goddess," I wheezed. "If that dog had caught us, it would have torn us apart."

"From the knees down, anyway," Da said, and we convulsed with laughter again.

Tomorrow I would need to talk to Celia and Robin.

On Wednesday, I was jolted awake by the ringing of the phone, which I had placed right next to my bed. I grabbed it without opening my eyes. "How did it go, my love?" I asked Morgan.

"Okay, I think," she said. "Did I wake you up?"

"It's all right. I was up a bit late last night. But I want to hear what happened."

"I don't think I dreamed," she said, uncertainty in her voice. "I can't remember anything, and I don't think I sleepwalked. But I feel yucky. Weird and uneasy, as if I saw something awful but I'm blocking it out."

"Hmmm. But you remember nothing?"

"No, nothing since I fell asleep. I just feel like I have a storm cloud hanging over my head. I don't know why."

"We're going to unravel this," I promised her. "Very shortly."

"I know," she said, sounding wan. "I'd better go—Mary K. has a pep club meeting before school."

"All right. Call me after school and we'll get together," I said. "I want to see you."

"Okay," she said.

After we hung up, I lay in my bed for a while, worrying about Morgan. I didn't know for certain what was going on with her dreams, but if it was that bastard Cal, come back to haunt her, I was going to destroy him. Somehow.

"Morning, all," said Da as he entered the kitchen about an hour later. His gray hair was recently trimmed, and the more time that passed, the more his rangy frame seemed to fill in.

"Da." I nodded.

"Morning, Uncle Daniel," said Sky. "Cuppa? I've got a pot made."

"Ta, lass," said Da.

"Say, Da," I said. "I've arranged to meet Celia and Robin—those two witches I told you about—downtown in half an hour. Since you know a bit about the case now, do you want to come?" I was happy to spend time with my father again, and truthfully, his quiet, matter-of-fact nature might help keep this meeting from being ugly.

"Yes, if I'm free," he said, taking his first sip of tea. "I'll need to check my book."

It still struck me as odd that my father was becoming so in demand as a speaker and teacher. I would always have that image of him as the emaciated hermit in Canada, as he'd been when I'd first found him. It seemed like he was metamorphosing in front of my eyes.

"There they are," I said in a low tone as we entered the coffee shop half an hour later. Once again Celia and Robin had taken the corner table, but unlike last time, the place was much more crowded. My father and I both ordered herbal tea.

"Hello, Celia. Hello, Robin," I said politely as we approached their table. "I hope you don't mind—this is my father, Daniel Niall. I've told him about your case, and I think he could be helpful to us. Da, this is Celia Evans and Robin Goodacre."

They all shook hands, and I was pleased and a little surprised that they recognized his name and looked impressed: the man who wrote the spell to conquer the dark wave.

"Last night my father and I visited Patrice's house," I began, and went on to tell them of what we'd found, the couple of poisonous plants mixed in with the herbs and vegetables. Both women looked concerned.

"Many plants are ornamental," Celia said, obviously looking for a loophole.

"You're right," I agreed, "and I certainly made allowances for that. What bothered me was the placement of the plants. They were in vegetable and herb beds, right next to edible plants that looked similar. Few of them were truly ornamental. In other words, I wasn't concerned about the row of rhododendrons lining her drive. You see the difference?"

Robin nodded reluctantly, and Celia clasped her hands around her glass and frowned.

"There's been no evidence of her trying to poison anyone," she said. "None."

I took a sip of tea. "I know—I'm not suggesting that she's poisoning anyone. It just struck me as interesting."

"Well, you're on the wrong track here," Celia said shortly.

I held up my hands in a placating gesture. "Look, I don't have any definitive answers at this point. It's important that I don't rule out any possibilities—even ones that are hard or ugly or not what you want to hear. I'm either looking for the truth or I'm not. Right?"

Celia set her jaw and deliberately uncoiled her fists. "I'm saying that I feel it's *highly* unlikely that Patrice could ever poison anyone."

"Right. And it *is* highly unlikely. But the only thing we can do is look at the whole picture, not just parts of it. Do you agree?"

"Yes. But the scenario you're describing is simply incompatible with Patrice as a person."

"Good," I said. "I would love to be able to tell you that your trust is completely well placed. I hope I can, once I've done more research."

"Well, what do we do now?" asked Celia. "We have a circle in two days."

"I need to investigate some more," I told them. "We can't do anything until we know for certain what's going on. It's possible that I'm completely misinterpreting the situation. It's possible that someone or something else is causing the strange fatigue after your circles. However, if Patrice is responsible, if she really is practicing dark magick . . . well, in most cases the witches are turned in to the council and stripped of their power."

"We can't have that," Celia said, and Robin shook her head. "Absolutely not," she agreed.

"There must be other options," Celia said. "Perhaps counseling, or an intervention, or simply removing her from her source of power."

"There are always options," I said mildly. "But it may be that Patrice's own actions will cause her options to be narrowed."

Celia and Robin were silent.

I glanced across at Da, who had been quiet and watchful during this whole exchange. He gave me an almost imperceptible nod, and I felt incongruously pleased.

"We need to think about this," said Celia.

"Please, don't do anything until we contact you again," Robin added. She grabbed her purse and stood, and Celia got up as well.

"We're not trying to be difficult or obstructive," Celia assured me. "It's just a complicated situation, and it seems to be getting more complicated. But we'll talk things over and give you some definite direction as soon as we can. Okay?"

I nodded. "I understand."

"Fair winds," Celia murmured as she and Robin brushed past me to the exit.

"And to you," I made the traditional reply.

My tea was now cold. I sighed and heated it up again with a quick circle of my hand.

"If she's working dark magick, our options just went down to one," Da said finally.

"Perhaps," I said. "But perhaps Celia and Robin are right: we can come up with something else. Somehow I don't want to turn her in to the council, not now. We're smart, Da. You're a brilliant spellcrafter. I have strongly honed skills and instincts. Surely between the two of us we can find a different solution."

"Well, we don't have to decide now," my father said, sipping his tea. "If they want you to continue, we'll just concentrate on gathering as much information as we need."

"Right."

9

Morgan

"Night, honey," Mom said. "Don't stay up too late."

"I won't," I said. She smiled and closed the door behind her. I was sitting up in bed, reading the Great Depression chapter in my history textbook—a little light reading to keep my mind off things. Well, I needed to study. And the truth was, I didn't want to go to sleep tonight. Bethany's potion had worked last night, as far as I knew. But I had still felt uncomfortable this morning, like something was off. All of my instincts were telling me that sleep was a bad idea tonight.

It had been so good to see Hunter this afternoon after school. He, Mary K., and I had all gone to the diner out on the highway and had milk shakes. It had seemed so normal, so reassuring. But now I was alone, it was bedtime, and my family was going to sleep around me.

As soon as I heard the door to my parents' room close and heard Mary K. get into her own bed, I put down my book and pulled out a slim magazine: *Green Gage,* a quarterly journal of modern Wicca. I loved their articles—in this issue there were recipes for light summery drinks and how to imbue them with magickal properties. There were features on summer gardening and on various crafts, like sewing, basket weaving, and spinning your own yarn.

When I cast out my senses, I found that everyone was asleep, probably having normal dreams about forgetting to study for a test, or that one that Mom had told me about, where she dreamed she sold the perfect house for a ton of money and when she proudly threw open the door for the new owners, it was a total wreck inside. Those were the kinds of dreams I could handle.

It was eleven-fifteen. My eyelids felt a little heavy, but I wasn't about to give myself over to sleep. I padded downstairs barefoot and got a glass of juice from the fridge. I took it into the family room, where the family computer was set up. Dad had recently gotten a cable modem and now we were always online and fast, fast, fast. I loved it.

I did a search for *dream magick/Wicca,* and that turned up some useful sites. Forty minutes later my eyes felt gritty and the glare of the computer screen in the dark room was giving me a headache. I still didn't want to dream, but if I took Bethany's potion now, it would surely knock me out safely. I clicked on one more Wiccan site and found a mention of a disclosure-type spell, one to reveal who was expending energy on you: people who were thinking a lot about you, working for you or against you, people who had strong emotions about you. I shrugged. It was worth a try. It wasn't like I'd found anything else.

I printed out the page and went up to my room. After a short internal struggle—was I ready to risk another dream?—I surrendered to exhaustion and gulped down the second half of Bethany's potion. It would take almost an hour to kick in. I would probably be a mess at school the next day, but oh, well. Inside my room I did a quick delay spell on the door, then got my magick-making supplies from my closet. I set out my four element cups and drew three circles of protection before casting the final circle. Then I sat cross-legged inside the circle and lit a single candle, invoking the Goddess and the God. I also gave thanks for everything in my life that was going well. I was learning that expressing gratitude for everything I possibly could helped dispel some of the negativity I picked up without even trying.

The page with the spell was on the ground next to me, and I read the words carefully. Some of them were in Gaelic, written out phonetically so that they were easy to pronounce. At the appropriate times I drew the runes Ansur, Eolh, Daeg, and Sigel in the air above the candle. Then, facing the candle, I pressed two fingers from each hand over my eyes and tried to see with my "inner eye," the one that sees reality with no interpretation.

Soon I saw Hunter's image, and followed by that, like a page flipping in a book, I saw Alyce's image and Bethany's—they were concerned about me and trying to help me. More faintly I saw my own family, who loved me but didn't seem actively worried about me, which was good. Then they faded away, and I saw the fuzzy outline of a shadow, huge and distorted on a wall. It became slightly clearer, darker, enough so that I could tell it was a person. I kept watching and once more murmured the words of the spell. As I watched, the shadow seemed to come away from the wall, becoming more three-dimensional, as if the shadow itself was assuming a form. Reveal yourself, I breathed. Reveal yourself.

As if from a distance the shadowy form contracted and

writhed and expanded. Finally it took on a form I could recognize: a hawk. *Another hawk!* Dumbstruck, I watched it fly away, and then I slowly opened my eyes.

Why couldn't I see who it had been? Was it Cal, as everyone seemed to think? How could he do this? I had felt his cold cheek—he had truly been dead.

I dismantled the circle and put my supplies away. In my readings I had learned that most Wiccans believed when someone died, their anam went to the netherland, a kind of holding place. In the netherland their life is reviewed, and a person can then choose to come back to this world in a new incarnation, ever working toward that spiritual perfection that will allow them to join with the Goddess as one. It was a nice idea. I had grown up believing in Catholicism's idea of heaven, and I could still see the appeal of a perfect resting place. But I liked Wicca's chance to come back again and try to do better with your life.

A few sources I had found discussed the ability of an anam actually to linger in the world without immediately going to the netherland. They had suggested that for an anam to retain any of its power or coherence, it had to have another vessel to reside in. It could be a literal vessel, like a metal box or glass jar with a lid—or in extreme cases it could be another person or even an animal. Like a hawk.

As soon as I had that thought, a cold chill washed over me. A *hawk*. Was there any way—oh, Goddess, I couldn't think about this. I was really getting paranoid. As Hunter said, hawks were all over the place, everywhere. The images of hawks in my dreams were probably representative of something else, like a generalized threat of some kind.

Okay. But what if it *was* a person doing this to me? These dreams seemed so personal. It would have to be someone who knew me, even knew me well, or at least could find out a great deal of personal information about me.

Ciaran? My natural father had had his powers stripped, so it couldn't be him. But what about other witches from Amyranth? How could I find out?

Killian.

It took me a minute to find my half brother's latest phone number and go back down to the family room. When I called, I got a disconnect message. I called information and got another number for him, and amazingly, when I called it, my half brother answered. On the seventh ring.

"Morgan! How lovely to hear from you!"

I couldn't help smiling. For all of Killian's character flaws, I couldn't help responding to his good nature, his affection, his unquenchable thirst for fun. And he apparently didn't hold a grudge: the last time I'd seen him had been in the old Methodist cemetery, our local power sink. I had trapped our mutual father there, and his powers had been stripped. Ciaran MacEwan had gone from being an incredibly powerful, charismatic, forceful, and evil witch to being a shriveled, powerless husk. Because of me.

"Hi, Killian," I said. "How are you?"

"Tops, sis, just tops. On my way out—the local watering hole does a bang-up microbrewery stout. The lads are waiting for me."

"I bet. And some lasses, too, no doubt."

Killian laughed.

"Listen, Killian," I said. "I was wondering—I haven't talked to you in a while, and I was hoping you could give me some news about Ciaran."

"Ah," he said, and I had a sudden image of a glass of champagne losing its bubbles. "Our sweet da. Well, sis, I won't lie to you. He has seen better days."

My heart gave a pang of remorse and guilt. "Where is he?" I asked softly.

"A type of rest home in Ireland," said Killian. "Down in Clonakilty, by the southern coast. It's warmer there. Relaxing. I hopped over to see him a fortnight ago. He hasn't really turned a corner yet, I'm afraid."

"I'm sorry." My throat felt tight as I experienced the usual dichotomy of emotions I felt about Ciaran. He had killed my birth mother. He had been one of the leaders of an incredibly evil dark coven, Amyranth. I knew he had personally caused any number of people to be killed, and he had, in fact, tried to kill me. But in an unexplainable psychological perversity, I had loved him and respected him. I had been very drawn to him, and oddly, he had seemed to sincerely care for me, though his love for power had definitely outweighed his love for me. Something in me resonated with something in him, and while that worried me, I also couldn't deny it. I cared about him. I didn't want him to die. But I hadn't been able to let him continue to work the appalling forms of dark magick he had loved.

"Tchah, Morgan," Killian said with unexpected gentleness. "I'm sorry for him, too, but Goddess, this is the threefold law barely coming home to roost. You didn't set him in motion. You only slowed him down a lot."

"Thanks," I managed to say. The knot in my chest loosened a bit.

"Besides," he went on. "What Mum's doing to him is making your bit look like child's play."

"Oh, Goddess. What's happening?"

"She's divorcing him," Killian said, and there was amusement in his voice. "An illegitimate child, untold dark workings, several very public affairs, years of fights and barely masked hatred and betrayal—none of these were enough to make Mum take this drastic step. But now that Da has no more power than a firefly, she's running him down."

"Oh, no," I said. I had been the illegitimate child.

"Well, it's a shame, but what goes around, comes around," Killian said lightly. I knew he cared for his father, but I also knew there was a great deal of anger and resentment there, too. Ciaran hadn't been a good father to anyone. And he'd treated his wife just as badly.

"Goodness. I wonder what's happening to Amyranth without him?" I made my voice casual, but from the pause on the other end I knew Killian wasn't fooled.

"Basically I think they're running around like chickens with their heads cut off," Killian said, deciding to answer me. "I haven't had any direct news, but from gossip I've picked up, I gather that Da had held his reins of power so tightly that no one was really waiting in the wings. It would take an incredibly strong witch to assume control, and knowing Da, he probably made sure there was no one that strong near the top."

"Huh. So what happens now?"

"Someone will eventually get their act together and step in. I predict lots of infighting and backstabbing," he said cheerfully. "It should be quite the soap opera for a while."

"Wow." So it didn't sound like either Ciaran or Amyranth

was together enough to be behind my dreams, then. "Well. What are you doing for Beltane? Anything planned?"

"I've had a couple of invites. What about you?"

"Oh, we're having a celebration here," I told him. "Food, drink, maypole, dancing."

"Say, what a great idea! That sounds terrific, and we can get all caught up," said Killian.

Ack! I thought. I could just picture Killian loping into our little Beltane celebration. It was going to be tense enough, with both Raven and Sky there, but to have the third member of the disastrous love triangle there would be too much. Either this thought hadn't occurred to Killian, or it had, and he simply assumed it wouldn't be a problem. But I hadn't even *invited* him!

"Um," I said, wondering how to put this. "Okay, but wear armor?"

"Great, then, Morgan. I'll see you Beltane Eve. Thanks so much for calling! Ciao!"

The phone line went dead before I could say anything. Jeez, I thought. What horrible emotional catastrophe had I set in motion? I shook my head and hung up the phone and then was hit by an unexpected giggle. Killian was really too much. I was knotted up by stress, yet Killian was living it up. Nothing seemed to get to him. It was oddly comforting.

Still smiling, I sat down on the family room couch and pulled a throw pillow into my lap. The house was dark around me, except for the glare of the computer screen and a small lamp on a side table. I could feel my family sleeping upstairs and lamented the fact that lately it always seemed that I was the only one who was up when everyone else was asleep.

I rested my head against the back of the couch, feeling like my arms and legs weighed a ton, like I was standing on Jupiter. I closed my eyes. Of course, I couldn't actually stand on Jupiter—it was mostly made of . . .

"Morgan. I've been waiting for you."

I jump. Oh, Goddess. This can't be real.

Cal is sitting right next to me. I'm struck with different feelings; the most disturbing is an actual gladness to see him. I felt terrible when he died, and something in me won't let me forget my first love. Then I feel the fear and mistrust sink in. My muscles tense, and adrenaline starts pumping into my system. Lastly I'm hit with overwhelming guilt—that I could feel glad to see Cal when I am so completely in love with Hunter.

"It's so good to see you," Cal says, his warm golden eyes probing mine. I feel dreamy, slowed. Part of me knows what to do, how to take charge of this situation, but most of me feels like just floating along, waiting to see what will happen.

"I've missed you so much, Morgan," he says earnestly. "You're very special to me. Together you and I can do wonderful things."

Struggling with my sleep-tied tongue, I manage to spit out, "I doubt it."

"No, no, it's true." Cal takes my hand and stands, pulling me up with him. Is this a dream, so I can use my guided-dreaming techniques? Or is it real? I can't tell, and it seems so hard to think about it, to concentrate. Cal's walking along, and now we're in a beautiful rolling meadow, dotted with wildflowers. The sun feels warm on my skin; I hear the soothing drone of bees as they buzz from flower to flower. The wind blows, fresh and cool, and at this moment it seems that everything is perfect.

But when I look ahead, it's Cal holding my hand, not Hunter. I pull back and frown. "No," I say.

Cal turns around, puzzled. "It's just up here a little bit. Not far. I've got a picnic waiting."

Some small part of my brain remembers my picnic with Hunter in the woods, how in love I felt, how close to him. "I don't want to go," I say, my bare feet stopping in the cool green grass.

Oddly Cal doesn't become angry or upset. Looking sympathetic, he comes to me and gently brushes my hair off my face. "I understand," he says. "But it'll be okay. It's just a little bit farther."

Inexplicably I begin walking again, letting him lead me on through this heavenly place. Is this what the netherland is like? Oh, Goddess, am I dead? For some reason this thought strikes me as funny, and I laugh, feeling the cool breeze on my face. I can't be dead—I have finals starting in two weeks! This makes me laugh more, and Cal turns around and smiles at me.

I look around, still being led by the hand like a child. Behind me is a dark line of trees, their leaves swaying gently. We're walking down a gentle slope, and I become aware of a rippling, gurgling brook. The idea of putting my bare feet into an icy stream sounds wonderful, and I walk on. It must be close.

"Here," says Cal. He stops and gestures proudly. I look up and see not a burbling stream, but Cal's bed. It's set up in front of me, a beautiful, dark four-poster bed, hung with a filmy mosquito net. When I first saw it, I thought it was the most romantic bed I had ever seen. For one moment I flash on Hunter's bed—his mattress and box spring on the floor in his room, his unmatched sheets, his threadbare comforter. . . .

I would rather be there, my mind insists.

"I don't want to be here," I say clearly, hearing my words drift away on the breeze.

"It's okay," Cal says soothingly. "I would never make you do

anything you didn't want to do. I've missed you. I just want to be with you."

I look at him, and his face is open, real, and as beautiful as I remembered. This face was the first to ignite desire in me, but those first sparks felt nothing like the rich, full longing I feel for Hunter. I pull my hand out of his.

"No," I say, more loudly. "This isn't what I want. I don't want to be here. I can't be with you, Cal."

His perfect brows arch downward. "I don't understand," he says. He takes my hand again and tugs me gently forward. "You love me. You want to be with me. I've always been the one you loved. I love you."

"No," I say again. "I didn't know any better then. But I do now."

He frowns, starting to look determined. "You'll never love anyone more than me," he insists. "You know we need to be together."

"That's not true," I say strongly, and pull my hand away again. I start to back away. I don't know how to get out of here. Dimly I remember something about guided dreaming? Interactive dreaming? But it doesn't make sense.

Cal comes and stands behind me, his hands on my shoulders. I feel the warmth of his touch through my long T-shirt.

Long T-shirt? What am I doing outside, dressed like this? This is what I sleep in—

"No!" I cry, wrenching my shoulders away from Cal's hands. Then suddenly the world goes black. I blink again and again, trying to focus. Where's the meadow? Why am I cold? Where am I? The sound of water is loud in my ears.

I looked down and sucked in a frozen breath. *Goddess!* I was outside, it was night, and I was standing on the rocky ledge where Cal and Hunter had fought, months ago! My toes could feel the unstable ground crumbling beneath me. This was where I had thrown an athame at Hunter, where I thought I had killed him. Now I was going to fall over the same cliff. My arms started to windmill in slow motion as I felt my weight start to shift over the ledge. Below me was a twenty-five-foot drop onto rocks, surrounded by icy mountain runoff.

I was going to die. Cal had led me here to die.

Small pebbles and dirt broke free beneath my feet, and I heard their almost imperceptible tumble down the cliff. Goddess, Goddess, help me, I thought, cold sweat breaking out on my forehead. I was going to die, right here, right now, unless I saved myself. I needed to save myself.

Holding my breath and going against every survival instinct I had, I consciously willed myself to relax every muscle. My feet were peddling against the side of the ledge. I felt my balance start to shift. Drop, I told myself, my eyes closed. Drop. Your weight will carry you backward. Just let yourself fall.

Like a building in an earthquake, my body went limp and I crashed heavily to the ground with a *thud*. Every bone in my body shook with the impact. The breath left my lungs in a whoosh, and for several seconds my mouth worked uselessly, trying to suck in air. I felt my feet dangling over the edge, and my eyes shot open. I turned over and scrabbled at the dirt and roots around me, finding one to latch onto. Holding the root, I snaked forward on my belly until I was sure I was on solid ground. There was a pine tree right there, and I crawled over to it, sitting curled up with my knees drawn up under my big T-shirt. I was filthy.

It was then that I allowed the rest of my consciousness to come to life. I shivered uncontrollably, partly because of the chill of the late-spring night and partly because it was hard to remember when I had last been so frightened. I had experienced plenty of danger in the last few months, but the reality of death, the possibility of dying without any of my loved ones understanding what had truly happened—it was terrifying. Cal had led me here in a dream. I looked around quickly, casting my senses, but didn't pick up on anything except the normal animal life of the woods.

Cal had led me here to kill me.

Suddenly my stomach roiled, and I got to my hands and knees. I dry-heaved for a minute, then curled up again, feeling the sickening crash of the adrenaline leaving my veins. I needed Hunter.

Hunter, come. Please help. Hunter! Help me!

Was he asleep? Had he heard me? Should I try Sky, or Alyce, or Bethany?

Coming.

Oh, thank the Goddess. Now I just had to keep it together until Hunter got here. Then I could turn into a shrieking, terrified banshee.

I couldn't estimate time—every minute felt like an hour—but finally I heard a car coming down the dirt road to the river's edge. When I recognized the familiar outline of Hunter's car and then felt his presence, I was too relieved to even stand up and go to him. Instead, I collapsed on the ground as he hurried over to me, and he put his arms around me.

10

Hunter

Hunter, come. Please help. Hunter! Help me! For a moment I didn't understand who was calling me, but then Morgan's voice pierced my brain, and I bolted awake. Within moments I was zipping up my jeans, pushing my feet into shoes, grabbing my jacket on the way out.

Coming, I sent back, practically leaping off the front porch. It was as black as a cave outside, and I had no idea what time it was. I looked at the moon, low on the horizon, and figured we weren't far from dawn.

Inside my car I started the engine, then remembered the message, thinking on where it had come from. I closed my eyes and recalled it. Bloody hell! The cliff by the river!

I poured on the speed, practically flying, not questioning why Morgan was there, only sure that it had been her voice. I found the old rutted road without difficulty and turned onto it. Finally, right by the cliff, my headlights illuminated Morgan's slender body, curled up in nothing but a dirty T-shirt under a tree. I threw myself out of the car and raced toward her.

"Goddess. My love, come here," I said, pulling her into my arms. I sat on the ground and held her in my lap. I wrapped my jacket around her and rubbed her arms and shoulders to warm her. She must be freezing. What the hell was she doing out here? Her bare feet were dirty, and her legs were scratched and damp. I knew I had to wait for her to calm down before I would get any answers. In the meantime I tried to keep my own panic and anger down.

"Hunter—" she began, her voice breaking on a sob.

"Shhh, shhh, my love. I'm here. You're safe now. You're completely safe." I stroked her back, sending waves of calm, soothing comfort. Finally she lay quiet and relaxed against my shoulder. I pushed her hair, damp with tears, away from her face and held her more closely.

Her voice, when it came, was so small, I could barely hear it.

"It was Cal," she said.

At that name a white-hot rage ignited in me, and I struggled to damp it down.

"What happened, my love?"

She shook her head. "I was at home. I wasn't sure I wanted to go to sleep, but finally I just got exhausted and took Bethany's potion, the other half. I went downstairs to the family room and called Killian. I thought maybe he might have heard something about Ciaran or Amyranth that could help me figure out what's happening."

I nodded.

"But he said Ciaran was a mess, in some witch rehab place in Ireland, and that Amyranth was falling apart without him. So I figured neither one of them could be doing this."

"Sounds like you're right," I said. "It was a good idea to call Killian. And what happened then? Do you remember?"

"I sat down for just a minute—I remember feeling really tired. But then I looked up, and Cal was there, right next to me."

My stomach knotted up, and I felt my jaw clench.

"He said, 'Come on,' and then we were walking through a meadow," Morgan continued. "We were outside, and it was daytime. I guess that's when I probably left the house." She gave a little shudder, and her voice sounded wobbly again. "We walked through that meadow, and it was so pretty. Cal was saying stuff to me, like he knew I loved him. . . ." She hung her head and gripped my jacket more tightly around her.

"It's all right, Morgan. It was a dream. Do you remember what happened then?"

"He . . . he wanted me to *join* him. I said no, I didn't want to be there. And he said he knew I loved him, and I said no, not anymore, or something like that. He started getting upset and trying to pull me closer, and I was trying to remember the interactive dreaming, but nothing would stay in my head." She shook her head in frustration.

"It's all right," I said again. "You did just fine."

She drew in a deep, shivery breath and went on. "Finally I think I shouted *no!* and pulled my hand away, and then everything went dark because I had woken up, and I was outside, and it was nighttime." She started sobbing again, and I tried to soothe her as best I could.

"When I realized where I was, I was standing at the very edge of the ledge over there." She pointed. "At the *very* edge. My feet were almost over, and I could feel myself losing my balance."

I was speechless. I had once gone over that ledge myself, and it had been a miracle that I hadn't died. As it was, I had cracked two ribs and been covered with massive bruises for weeks. The water was lower now, since the mountain snowmelt hadn't been under way for long. If Morgan had gone over, I would now be looking for her battered body. I felt like I had been punched and very slowly tried to suck in a breath.

Cal had done this.

I blinked several times, using every bit of self-control I had to not give in to my fury. It was made a thousand times worse by the gripping panic I felt at how close Morgan had come to dying.

"What happened then?" I asked, my voice raspy and dry.

"I was about to fall. I could feel the dirt breaking away under my feet. I was so tense, I was sure I was going to lose my balance and fall forward. Finally I did a calming spell to relax my body and then let myself fall backward."

I tightened my hold on her, pressing her head against my chest and hugging her with all the relief and gratitude I felt.

"*Fuh*-uh," came her voice, and I realized I was crushing her. Instantly I relaxed my hold.

"I'm sorry," I said.

"It's okay," she said, drawing a deep breath. "I'm glad you're here." She looked up at me, her hazel eyes wide and red rimmed from crying. She still looked incredibly beautiful, with that strength I always saw in her.

She gave me a watery smile. "What time is it?"

I glanced at the horizon. "Looks like the sun's about to come up."

"I've got to get home," she said, looking at me with wide eyes. "My parents will be up any second!"

I nodded.

I parked one house down from hers, and we sat for a minute, casting out our senses.

"I'm not getting much," I said. "But it's still only five till six."

"I don't feel much, either," she said, sliding out of my jacket. "I guess I'll risk it. This is one day I won't have to rush to get ready for school."

"Tell them you were getting the newspaper," I suggested, pointing at the paper on the front walk.

Morgan gave an ironic snort, glancing down at her soiled T-shirt and feet, then kissed me quickly and opened her door.

"Morgan, this will end today," I said. "No matter what. As soon as I think Alyce is up, I'll call her and Bethany. Come to Practical Magick today after school. We'll be there, and we won't leave till we have a plan."

She gave me a wan little smile, then ran up the cold front walk. She paused for a moment in front of the door, then carefully eased it open. Seconds later her hand came back outside, its thumb pointing up. Everything was fine. Her parents would soon be up, and Mary K. was awake. Reluctantly I started my engine and headed for home.

Back home I went straight to my room. For almost half an hour I just lay on my bed, staring at the ceiling. Morgan had almost died because of Cal. I had to get a grip and then get to work with a cool head and a strong will. Finally I got up and started flipping through piles of books, looking for something that I could use to stop him. It was clear Cal's anam had somehow survived. I guessed that bastard had been stronger than I thought. Obviously he just couldn't get over the idea that Morgan loved someone else and that the someone else was me, his hated half brother. But now he wanted her so badly that he was willing to *kill* her to be with her? The thought was unbearable.

At seven-thirty I called Alyce and told her everything. She was horrified and also astonished that it had happened despite Bethany's sleep potion. She agreed this was too serious to continue for another day and said she'd meet us at four that afternoon. I asked her to call Bethany and tell her what had happened, and she said she would.

Downstairs I found Sky in the kitchen, an unusually sour look on her face.

"What's wrong?" I asked, pouring myself a cup of tea.

She sighed and shook her head. "I called some members of Kithic to talk about Beltane," she said. "I thought I could get the ball rolling on the celebration. Everyone seemed gung ho. So I started making plans yesterday—thinking about fresh flowers, oatcakes with honey, where to get a maypole."

"Sounds good," I said.

"You would think so," she said tartly. "Unfortunately, what no one told me was that someone *else* had also started working on plans for Beltane."

I frowned. "I hadn't heard about that. Who?"

Sky gave me an icy stare. "Raven."

I took a drink of my tea to allow myself time to formulate a response. On the one hand, I almost felt like saying, Well, you know what? Morgan almost died this morning. But on the other hand, I knew how much Sky had been hurt by her breakup with Raven, and she was my cousin and I loved her and didn't want her to be hurt.

"Crap," I said inadequately, then realized with no small amount of horror that I had picked up that expression from Morgan.

Sky looked at me with raised eyebrows. "Raven called here last night, incensed," she continued. "I can't just waltz back into town and start messing with her plans and so on. So we barked at each other for a while, and neither of us would back down, and then we had a better-idea-than-thou contest."

"Who won?"

"Neither of us," Sky admitted. "As hard as it is to believe, she actually had one or two decent ideas."

"Hmmm. So what happens now?"

Sky gave a heartfelt sigh and stretched her arms over her head, arching her back. "Well, unfortunately, my brain tumor chose to act up just then, and I agreed to meet Raven in person to discuss ideas." She shook her head, her feathery white-blond hair flying. "I don't know what I was thinking. All I can do now is hope that I'm hit by a stomach flu."

I looked at my cousin with interest. Morgan was strong, and Sky was also strong, but in a different way. Morgan was strong like a young willow tree, able to bend with the storm. Sky was strong like a knife. It was extremely unusual for her to admit any kind of weakness whatsoever. For her to tell me that she would rather get horribly sick than see Raven was a clue as to how raw her feelings still were. Sky could be quite ruthless—all she had to do was call Raven and cancel. But she wasn't planning to do so. It was very interesting and also a little alarming.

Sky looked at me looking at her and got an irritated look on her face. "Oh, shut up," she muttered, standing and carrying her plates to the sink. I waited till she left before I groaned quietly.

Later I found my father in our circle room, hunched over an old tome that looked like it was disintegrating right before my eyes.

"You were up early, lad," he said, looking at me over the half-moon reading glasses he had recently started wearing.

I told him everything that had happened this morning with Morgan, and his face became increasingly concerned. It was hard for me to moderate what I said about Cal and his suspected involvement, but Da hid his reaction, if he had any.

"Bad news, son," he said when I was done. "Do you think Alyce and Bethany have a handle on it?"

"Yes," I said. "We're all doing research, and I think we're pulling a plan together tonight."

"I see. Is there something I could do to help?"

His voice sounded a little stiff, and I knew there was no way he could remain objective about Cal.

"No, Da, I don't think so."

"Right, then. Well, let me know." He paused. "In the meantime, I've been thinking about Patrice." He took off his glasses and tapped the book with them. "There's some interesting reading here. It talks about some variants of common limiting spells that seem to have interesting possibilities. Of course, I'm afraid Patrice is in all probability going to end up getting her powers stripped."

"I hope not," I said. "Let's just keep trying to be creative."

I told him about some of the reading I had done lately, a few histories of witches who had, by accident, been the victims of spells that had gone awry. There had been one witch who had surprised herself by losing her powers in January—only in January—but in every January after that, for the rest of her life. Things like that. Another had lost the ability to work any kind of animal magick, but only animal magick.

Da looked intrigued, and I told him I would show him my sources.

"It's an interesting problem," he said, putting on his glasses and turning back to his book. "Very interesting."

11

Morgan

When school was over, Mary K. met me by Das Boot and we headed for home. I felt foggy and distant, and I could barely remember anything that had happened that day. However, as awful as I had felt, being surrounded by hundreds of other students hadn't been a bad thing. I had felt safe, lost in the hustle and bustle of classes and lunch and more classes.

"Yoo-hoo," Mary K. said loudly, and my head snapped in her direction. "I *said*, do you think you can give me a ride to Alisa's later?"

"Sorry," I said. "Didn't hear you. Um, I don't think so. I'm going to be home for just a minute, then Hunter's coming over and we're going out. Maybe Alisa can get a ride to our house."

"Okay, I'll ask."

At home I went up to the bathroom and tried to salvage my appearance somewhat. There wasn't a heck of a lot I could do. I stood in front of the mirror, feeling depressed and wondering if Hunter was legally blind. I felt Mary K. come up and sighed.

"Yeah, you're not exactly the poster child for glowing health, are you?" she said, leaning against the door frame.

"No, guess not." I turned to go, but my sister stopped me.

"Hold on a minute." She rummaged through her bathroom drawer and then held my face in a hard grip while she dabbed and brushed and stroked and almost blinded me with a mascara brush when I blinked.

"I'm going to look like a clown," I said warningly.

"No, you're not," she said. "Look."

I turned to the mirror, and once again my sister had managed to somehow work with my unpromising raw materials. My cheeks looked healthily pink, my eyes larger and more distinctive, and my mouth looked natural instead of looking like I had just donated a lot of blood. Yet I didn't even look made up. I looked like me, but me on a *really* good day.

"Nice?" she asked, obviously pleased.

"You are my idol," I said, staring at myself. "This is great."

Mary K. grinned, and then the phone rang and she went to answer it. I quickly changed my shirt, since I had spilled Diet Coke on it at lunch, and then Mary K. tapped on my door. "For you," she called. "It's someone named Ee-fuh or something like that."

Eoife. That's strange, I thought, taking the phone. "Hello?"

"Morgan," said Eoife McNabb's familiar voice. Instantly I pictured her in my mind: she was small, probably not much more than five feet tall. Her eyes were a warm, light brown, and her hair was the most shocking shade of natural red I had ever seen. "Hello, how are you?"

"Okay, I guess," I said warily. I liked Eoife and respected

her, but that didn't mean I trusted her completely. She was one of the subelders of the council.

"Morgan, do you have a moment? I need to talk to you about something."

"Um," I said, glancing at my watch. Hunter should be here any minute.

"I've been talking to some of the witches at Dùbhlan Cuan, the retreat where our most talented and knowledgeable teachers are, up in northern Scotland. The short story is, they've agreed to accept you as a probationary student this summer."

She sounded incredibly excited.

"Hm!" I said.

"It would be an intensive eight-week course. You would have to pay your airfare, but everything else, room and board, would be covered. Morgan, this is the first time any American witch has been accepted for teaching, much less one as young as you and as relatively untrained, uninitiated. It's the chance of a lifetime, one that many, many witches can only dream of. You would be foolish not to take it."

"Why did they accept me?" I asked. Eoife hadn't even told me she was going to put in an application.

"Because of your power," Eoife said simply. "A witch like you comes along only once every several generations. Morgan," she said gently. "I really think these could be the most important eight weeks of your life. The summer session starts in mid-June and lasts until mid-August. Please tell me you'll come."

All kinds of thoughts were flying through my head. Bree and I had a tradition of driving over to the Jersey shore for a beach vacation. That would be out, and so would long summer evenings eating snow cones, all the dumb summer movies. It would mean I couldn't work and earn money this summer, money that I always depended on to supplement my pitiful allowance throughout the year.

On the other hand, Hunter was going to be in England during the summer. I hadn't even been able to think about the pain of that separation and how much I dreaded it. If I was up in Scotland, it would be easier to see him. And the idea of being in an all-witch environment, where everyone understood me, where no one was suspicious, sounded like heaven. I would learn so much.

"I would love to," I said at last, and immediately sensed Eoife's relief. "The problem is, I'll need to ask my parents. If I was going over there to study math, they would be packing my bags. But to study Wicca—it's not going to go over well." My heart began sinking as soon as I said that.

"I see," said Eoife. "Yes. That could be a problem. Do you think it would help if *I* talked to them?"

I thought about it. More likely that conversation would be an unmitigated disaster. "Um, well, let me try asking them first. I'll let you know as soon as I can—and I'll really try to get them to agree. I really, really want to go."

"I'm glad," said Eoife. "Please do try, and let me know if it will help for me to talk to them. I'll call you soon for news, all right?"

"Yes. Thanks, Eoife. I really appreciate it." We hung up and I hurried downstairs just as I sensed Hunter coming up the walk.

He smiled when he saw me, his eyes examining me for signs of my horrible ordeal last night. We said good-bye to Mary K., and I grabbed my jacket.

"So, horrible stress agrees with you," he said as we walked to his car. "You look like you just took a brisk walk in the fresh spring air."

I shrugged, feeling pleased. "Hunter, you'll never believe what just happened," I said, and on our way to Red Kill, I told him all about Eoife's amazing offer.

Hunter looked more and more astounded, and when we parked in front of Practical Magick, he leaned over and hugged me hard. "Morgan! That's brilliant! It's like winning the Nobel Prize as a teenager! Goddess, I'm so proud of you!" He looked at me, his hands on my shoulders, and I smiled somewhat self-consciously. "Have you asked your parents yet?"

"No—they're not home, and Eoife just called. I'll ask them soon, when I find a really good moment."

"It would be an amazing, incredible experience," he said. "I hope they let you take it."

We got out of the car and headed into the store. "Does Mary K. know?"

"I didn't have time to tell her. You came right then, and she was headed to Alisa's house. She's agreed to go to Alisa's dad's wedding."

"Good. I'm hoping they can work things out."

Alyce came forward to meet us and took both my hands as an interested young customer watched us. "Come into the other room," she said quietly. "Bethany's already here."

Alyce had moved another table and more chairs into the back room where Hunter worked. Because the room had a door that closed, it felt more private than the little back kitchen, which had only a curtain.

Again, I told them everything I could remember about my

dream the previous night. I was already starting to forget details, and Hunter added things that I had told him when he'd first found me.

"To me, based on the things Cal was saying, it sounds like he simply can't let go of Morgan, can't accept that he's no longer part of her life," Hunter said, trying not to show how angry he was. "It's like he wants her with him."

"That could definitely be part of it," Bethany said. "But I think there's more to it than that. All the images of the fire-winged hawk—that's a common symbol for an uncommon person, a *sgiùrs dàn*."

Ciaran had called me a *sgiùrs dàn*, I remembered, but I hadn't known what to make of it.

"That's what I found out also," Hunter said. "And *sgiùrs dàn* basically means destroyer."

My eyebrows raised.

Alyce went on. "The research I've done in the last few days has turned up some interesting facts. First, the idea of the *sgiùrs dàn* seems particular only to the Woodbanes. The rough translation of the actual words is something like 'scourge of fate.' But the references to it I found made it sound more like the Indian Siva, something that destroys or wipes clean but also clears a path for new beginnings."

"And I'm one?" I asked, my voice practically squeaking.

Alyce looked at me and took a deep breath. "Possibly," she said. "I don't know why Ciaran would lie about that. In Woodbane history there are mentions of *sgiùrs dàns* every few generations. They're almost always women, and it seemed that after they've lived, or because of them, the course of Woodbane history changes."

"It could be coincidental," Hunter suggested. "A particularly charismatic or powerful witch comes along, and then they later attribute the change to her, identifying her as a *sgiùrs dàn* after the fact."

"Which doesn't explain why Morgan would be called one," said Bethany.

"I can't really find a connection to Morgan," Alyce admitted. "The last one seemed to be noted in 1902, and one source I found believes that person cleared the way for the creation of Amyranth."

"Great," I muttered, feeling a headache coming on.

"And then there was one back around 1820 or so," Alyce went on. "The *sgiùrs dàn* seems to be either light or dark, with no discernible pattern." She gave a sudden smile. "We're hoping you're light."

I made a thanks-a-lot face. "And this relates to me how?"

"We don't know," Alyce admitted. "It's just that you had dreams with images of a hawk that had wings made of fire. The only references we could find of that image were related to the *sgiùrs dàn*."

"At any rate, what's become quite clear is that these are definitely attacks against Morgan, and they're increasing in danger. They're now life-threatening, and they must be stopped," said Hunter.

"I agree," said Bethany.

"We have a plan," said Alyce, surprising me. She glanced across at Bethany. "We were working on it until late last night, and then today we think we've finished it—almost. The dreams are getting more realistic, more cohesive. I feel, and Bethany agrees, that there is a being behind this, probably

Cal Blaire, though we're not totally certain. My theory is that as the dreams become more cohesive, so does this being, or this anam. The dreams are leading up to a climax: Morgan's death. The presence, for lack of a better word, is finding that it has to keep upping its power, upping the tricks it uses on Morgan."

"A witch who wasn't strong as Morgan probably wouldn't have made it this far," Bethany said.

"What's your plan?" Hunter asked.

"A magickal trap," Alyce said. "Our idea is that as the being becomes more cohesive, it also becomes more vulnerable to being caught. If Morgan didn't take any sleeping potion and allowed herself to dream, I feel that this presence—"

"Cal," Hunter supplied.

"—would take that opportunity to launch its final attack. We three would be watching, hidden magickally. If Morgan sleepwalks, we'll follow her. If the presence shows up, we'll trap it."

"How do you catch an anam?" I asked.

"The three of us will join our powers and hold it in a binding spell," Bethany explained. "We'll adapt it for an amorphous being, but I feel that the three of us should be able to hold on to just about anything."

"At that point we'll ensnare it—"

"Cal," said Hunter.

"—in a piece of brown jasper, using a spell I've adapted from one I've read," Alyce went on, continuing to ignore Hunter's interruptions. "Then, after we question the anam, the crystal can be destroyed in any number of ways."

I thought this through. I didn't like the idea of sleeping

with no potion at all, but the idea that these three witches, whom I trusted so implicitly, would be right there, made it seem more doable.

"Okay," I said firmly, leaning forward. "I'm ready. Let's do it tonight. I appreciate all the work you've done," I said to the three of them.

"We're happy to help," Alyce assured me. "Now—we need a few hours to prepare and get set up. Morgan, I think you should just go home, have a light dinner, then come back to my apartment around eight. Will there be a problem with school?"

I frowned, then shook my head. "I'll tell my parents I'm sleeping over at Bree's. They usually don't mind."

"Fine, then. Hunter and Bethany, can you stay here so we can go over things again?"

"Let me just run Morgan home, then I'll be right back," Hunter said. They agreed, and as Hunter drove me home, I felt more optimistic than I had in days.

12

Hunter

I was on my way back to Practical Magick when Celia called me on my mobile. "We just heard—Patrice has asked us to move our usual Friday circle to this afternoon because Joshua is undergoing tests tomorrow."

"Why doesn't Patrice just ask someone to step in?" I asked pointedly.

"She never likes substitutes," Celia said, her tart tone telling me she had gotten my point. "Can you come? This would be a good chance to observe a circle."

I glanced at my watch and remembered that I had my magickal gear in a backpack in the boot of my car. "I'm in the middle of something crucial," I said, "but let me check, and I'll call you right back."

I spoke to Alyce, and she agreed that if I could get back there by eight o'clock, it should be fine. We'd have to explain the entire plan to Morgan, anyway.

"Right," I said. "If I can make it earlier, I will." Then I called Celia back. "I'm on my way," I said, and Celia gave me directions.

Many covens meet in someone's house or outdoors. It was somewhat unusual to have Kithic move from house to house, the way it did, and Willowbrook also was a little unusual in that it rented commercial space.

In Thornton, I parked my car about three blocks away from the address Celia had given me. They were starting their circle early, at five. I slipped on my backpack, then made my way toward the small, three-story building whose top floor Willowbrook rented. I made note of alleys, escape routes, which buildings connected where, which streets ran between what. By about quarter of seven I was in back of Willowbrook's building. There was a rusty fire escape ladder about two feet above my head. I gauged its condition, cast a quick see-me-not spell, and then jumped hard, catching the bottom rung and quickly clamping my other hand above that. A bit of hand-over-hand, and then my right foot caught the bottom rung.

One story up, the ladder attached to a small, rusted metal balcony that ran in front of two windows. Another staircase ran up to the third floor, and then a ladder went to the roof. I cast out my senses, then crept closer to the two windows I would have to pass. They led to a hallway with some employees starting to take off for the day. I scrambled up the staircase as fast as I could. Then a step across nothingness to the last ladder, and voilà, I was on the roof.

It felt like old days—by coincidence I was dressed all in dark gray, useful for reconnaissance, and I surrounded myself with the strongest cloaking spells I knew. No one would detect my presence. Up on the roof, I padded around until I felt I was right over Willowbrook's rooms. Robin had told me that their space included a one-room library, a tiny

kitchen, one room of storage, and a larger circle room.

Inside my backpack I had all my Seeker tools—some magickal things, but also some gadgets I had gotten at mail-order spy stores. Now I opened a small, foam-lined case and took out my tiny periscope. It was basically similar to the cardboard one Sky had made to spy on me when we were little, only this one was well made and spelled.

Slowly I lowered it down over the side of the building, grateful that their circle room overlooked the back of the building rather than the front, by the street. I said a little enhancement spell as it went down and hung over the edge so I could see exactly where the periscope was going.

As soon as it was maybe half an inch below the top of one window, I stopped and fitted my eye to the eyepiece. I rotated and zoomed and soon had a stellar view of the circle room. The room was painted a deep, rich purple. Crimson curtains hung on either side of an attractive altar lined with candles, incense, and silver cups filled with fresh flowers appropriate to the season. An embroidered cloth hung down on both sides of the altar, and I could see sigils for the Goddess and God. Nothing looked pretentious or fancy or flavored by wealth or pride. There were no obvious traces of dark magick. It was a circle room I would have felt comfortable in.

Turning my scope, I was able to count seven women (including Celia and Robin) and two men so far. I knew there were seventeen witches in all in the coven, but I assumed several of them wouldn't be able to make it at this unusual time and on such short notice. A minute later a woman came in, wearing a bright yellow robe: Patrice. She smiled

and greeted everyone, and though I cast my senses strongly, I couldn't pick up on anything like fear or mistrust or anger. Of course, they were mostly blood witches, and they could hide their feelings easier than most. But I got genuine warmth, affection, and caring, both to and from Patrice.

Right at five Patrice invoked the Goddess and the God and, with a simple, elegant, and heartfelt ceremony, dedicated the circle to the four elements. Then the ten present members joined hands and began some familiar chants: to raise power, to join and mingle their energies, to recognize spring, to acknowledge the Goddess. Each phrase had a wealth of meaning and a subtlety I appreciated. The members raised their linked hands above their heads and began to move deasil around the large room. The way they chanted told me that most of them had been together a long time, years, and were intimately familiar with the forms of the ceremony and with each other.

My nose wrinkled. This was an old building, and the sun of the spring day had released some acrid scent from the old-fashioned pitch that sealed crevices on the room. My knees already ached, and I shifted positions. All part of the job. I was thirsty and realized with annoyance that I had left my water bottle down in my car. Damn.

I watched Patrice in particular—she was attractive for an older woman, I saw now, something I hadn't picked up on when Da and I had scried before. She had medium brown hair streaked with lighter shades and dark blue eyes. She looked vibrant and intelligent, but also fatigued and tense.

The circle went totally normally, as far as I could tell, over the next half hour. When their chanting slowed, many coven

members shared things about their lives, or asked for help with a certain thing, or asked questions they hoped others could answer. I couldn't detect any reticence or mistrust. It was odd. Patrice really felt like the warm, caring, generous woman that Celia and Robin had described. But they couldn't deny their concerns.

Once again the ten witches joined hands and began moving deasil, beginning the final power chant, the one that should leave them feeling energized and peaceful for the next couple of days. Patrice began it, and one by one the other witches joined in, their sopranos, altos, tenors, and basses all weaving together like a tapestry of sound. To my eyes, Celia and Robin and perhaps two or three others looked a tiny bit hesitant, but no one refused to participate. Everyone joined in, and like a well-rehearsed choir, their voices fitted seamlessly together in a beautiful expression of the joy of magick.

This was confusing. I just didn't see what had concerned Celia and Robin, yet I had trusted their instincts and feelings. Was this the one night Patrice was going to skip whatever it was that had made them nervous?

But wait. I frowned and angled my little scope so I could once again see the whole circle. A new note had entered the song, a thin line of meaning underlying and circling and flitting in and out among the other voices. Quickly I determined that it was Patrice's full, attractive voice—and just as quickly my eyes opened wide as I recognized her song as one of the basic forms of a "hypnotic" spell. Her dark blue eyes seemed a bit more focused on the coven members as she sang. Over the next two minutes the other witches slowly began to seem glassy-eyed. All of them, including

Celia and Robin, were smiling, moving comfortably, keeping pace with the circle, continuing their song in a kind of circular reel that often helps invoke the most energy.

Patrice wasn't even pretending now to be part of the power chant. She held hands with two members and kept moving in a circle, but she wasn't singing and her eyes were clear and intent. Her mouth had lines of tension around it, and her face looked more set than it had earlier. In the next moment I saw her lips move in an actual spell, and I cast my senses as strongly as I could to make out what she was saying.

Oh, Goddess. My mouth opened and I held my breath, training the scope on Patrice, zooming in so I could see her closely. I wasn't mistaken. Patrice was casting a spell on the coven, a spell that would gather the energy they were raising now and refocus it on her so that she would absorb all of it. Not only that, but some of the phrasing she was using indicated that this would gather not only the energy raised here and now, but also whatever energy could be pulled without too much force from each person there.

This was dark magick. If Patrice had been ill herself and had asked her covenmates to direct energy toward her, to aid in her healing, that would be fine. People did that all the time. This was deliberately taking something not offered from a living being, doing it without permission. To hypnotize an entire coven and sap their energy was completely wrong, and any initiated witch would know that.

After several minutes Patrice once again joined her voice into the power chant, and I heard her weave a spell of forgetfulness, of trust, of safety into the last round. Then voices raised to a crescendo. I looked up quickly to see that the sun was just setting at this instant, that it had gotten dark as I had sat on the roof, and my knees were completely numb from being knelt on for two hours.

My eye back on my scope, I watched as the last note was cried. Instantly each witch sank to the ground, crouching on their hands and feet, as if to ground themselves. This was unusual. I hadn't seen a coven do this before. I looked at Patrice and saw that she was hunched over, her shoulders shaking, her head bobbing. I assumed she had absorbed so much excess energy that she felt sick and needed time to assimilate it. At least four of the witches on the ground seemed to be leaning against others, as though they would fall over without support. Robin was also hunkered down on all fours, her shoulders heaving as if she felt ill.

I shook my head. Having your energy taken from you against your will is an ugly thing. No wonder Celia and Robin had forced themselves to overcome their loyalty and trust of Patrice to seek out help. Patrice had driven them to extraordinary lengths.

Slowly people began looking up, either sitting down cross-legged or trying shakily to stand. Two women walked unsteadily to the kitchen and reappeared a few minutes later with fruit, fruit juice, tea, and cake. They put these on the floor, and witches literally scooted or crawled over to them, helping themselves to the food. This was horrible. Virtually every coven has snacks after a circle—there's something about making magick that seems to deplete one's blood sugar—but to see these initiated witches on the ground, too weak to stand up, turned my stomach. The food helped them, however. After eating and resting, they began standing up, grinning sheepishly at each other, as if embarrassed to be left so weakened by a circle. Patrice was the last one to stand, and I saw Celia and Robin watching her.

When she stood up and I saw her face, I saw that she too had been transformed by the circle, but in quite a different way than her coven. She looked terrific, as if she'd just had sixteen hours' sleep. She seemed to be glowing with good health and energy, while all the others still seemed a bit wobbly and sluggish.

I had seen enough. I sat back and folded up my scope and was just putting it in its case when the back of my neck prickled.

"What are you doing up here?" a man's voice demanded.

I turned around and gave a nonchalant nod. He was obviously the janitor. "Cable guy," I said in an American accent, patting my little case. I glanced around, and bless the Goddess, there was actually a black cable running right by my feet. I took out a pair of wire strippers and picked up the cable in a professional matter. "Emergency call. It's too much to let a guy eat dinner, right?" Go away. Everything's fine. Someone on the second floor has called about a dripping sink.

"Oh," said the man. "Okay. Lock the access door when you leave."

"Will do," I said, not looking up. As soon as he closed the access door behind him, I stowed everything in my small backpack and shimmied down the ladder to the fire escape. Within seconds I was walking briskly to my car. The neighborhood was quiet and approaching twilight.

The truth was, I didn't know what I was going to do. If I were still a Seeker, I would recommend that Patrice be stripped of her powers. But I wasn't a Seeker, and I had promised Celia and Robin to try to think of some other less drastic way to stop Patrice. What Patrice was doing was egregiously wrong—no question. But Celia and Robin seemed so certain that Patrice was, in fact, a good person at heart, just someone who had been pushed to do extraordinary things because of difficult situations.

I would have to find another option.

I waited in my car until I saw Patrice's car pass mine. As soon as she did, I frowned: Robin was with her. Maybe Patrice was just giving her a ride home. But there was something about the tilt of Robin's head—I couldn't pin it down, but something felt off to me. After a minute I pulled out and followed her, keeping a good distance between us.

I followed Patrice to a state park not far from there called Highgate Woods. I hung back far enough to make sure Patrice didn't pick up on my presence, then followed her into the parking lot. There were maybe twelve other cars here, people jogging, walking dogs, but nowhere did I see Patrice's SUV. I parked and got out, strolling past every car, mentally doing reveal spells so that if Patrice had set some kind of magickal camouflage on her car, I would notice it. But though I circled the lot twice, I saw no sign of Patrice or Robin or the car.

This couldn't be—I had followed her right into the park, right past the welcome center, dammit. Had there been another turnoff there?

I sprinted back to my car and started the engine. Rookie move, Niall, I thought as I wheeled my car around and headed for the park entrance again. I went slowly this time, and there was, in fact, another turnoff. And beyond that were another two forks. I swore under my breath. I was wasting time I couldn't afford. Though I cast my senses, I couldn't detect Patrice's signature and so had to search the other two turnoffs by sight. Of course, she wasn't at the first parking lot I checked—that would have been too easy. I retraced my route again and tried the right turnoff. This time, among the few other cars parked there, I saw the SUV.

I jumped out of my car and then pawed through my backpack and took a number of things I might need. I strode quickly to the park's entrance and cast my senses for Patrice, turning up nothing. No surprise. I searched for Robin, counting on the fact that Patrice probably wouldn't have thought to cover her tracks. This time I got something and headed into the park, down one of the maintained trails.

Although it was rapidly growing dark, I soon sensed that Robin had left the trail and set off cross-country. If I hadn't had to backtrack so much, I'd have been able to see them ahead of me. As it was, I relied on my senses and realized that the deeper I got into the woods, the more I could actually pick up on a trail of magick. Of course, I expected confusion spells, misdirection spells, and so on, but just the pattern of those spells themselves, where they were placed, what area they covered, was enough for me to triangulate a location. A more experienced witch—or a witch in less of a hurry—would have done a much better job of covering her path.

Besides the lingering prickles of magick I felt around me, I also saw signs that someone—two someones—had been through here recently. And they hadn't been careful about not leaving their mark all over the vegetation. A snapped twig here, the scrape of lichen there. It was a pretty clumsy show. I quickly considered the possibility that there were fake signs, created to mislead me, but I didn't feel that they were. The whole thing felt almost amateurish.

Here in the protected part of the woods, it was almost completely without light and more thickly vegetated. Once again I felt some misdirection spells. They were like tissue paper—I was walking right through them. Good thing Patrice hadn't set up the ones my da had used in Canada—the ones where everything in you is screaming uncontrollably that you'll die a horrible, painful death if you take one more step. Though I had managed to get through those, too.

After another minute or so I stopped and concentrated on Robin's energy pattern. I had never touched Patrice and so wouldn't recognize hers, but I did pick up Robin's, a bit more strongly this time. I turned about ten degrees to the north and set off again, stepping over fallen trees, pushing through thick undergrowth that waved leafy, twiggy branches in my face.

Soon I picked up on some disturbing feelings, of being upset, of fear, of feeling lost. More spells. It was actually rather amazing that Patrice had had enough time to do all of this, considering that she didn't seem experienced in terms of dark magick—plus the fact that I was only a few minutes behind her. All this had taken time. Unless she had set it up beforehand, and I didn't think she had. I told myself it wasn't real, that my mind knew the truth, and just bashed on, regardless. It was the only way to get through.

Though the early evening air was brisk, a chill sweat trickled down the back of my shirt. The air felt stale and muggy, making it difficult to breathe. Patrice's spells were a constant irritant, making me impatient. I damped down all these emotions. Emotions only clouded things in magick.

I stopped quietly when I realized I was close. Slowly I stepped forward, a foot at a time, as silently as I knew how. I crouched down on a small patch of damp leaves that wouldn't crinkle noisily under my weight. By edging a bush's branch down, I could see about fifteen feet ahead, to a very small clearing.

Robin was propped against a young sycamore tree, looking lifeless. Her head hung awkwardly to one side, strands of untamable auburn hair falling over her face. Her eyes were mere slits and had no consciousness flickering in them. Bloody hell.

Patrice was a few feet in front of Robin, wearing her yellow robe. I'd refreshed my earlier cloaking spells, and it was clear she had no idea I was there. Leaning over, she began to trace sigils and runes in the air above Robin's head. In her left hand she held a book that looked so old, its pages were brown and crumbling. I realized Patrice was crying as she continued the spell.

I listened hard and heard Patrice saying, "I'm sorry, I'm so sorry, Robin. I don't want to do this, but I have to. I don't know any other way. Please forgive me, Goddess forgive me." Sobs distorted her words. It was the strangest sight I'd ever seen, and that was saying something. I'd never seen someone working dark magick, causing harm to another, but feeling such regret about it at the same time.

From the form of the spell I could tell that Patrice was still working the limitations. From the form of the limitations it was clear that this spell was designed to sap Robin's life energy in a very strong way—such a strong way that I doubted whether Robin would survive. Maybe an incredibly strong witch might, but not Robin.

I took fifteen seconds to settle on a plan and picked an old favorite: the element of surprise.

With no warning I burst through the bush, racing toward Patrice, the *braigh* in my hand. She whirled, stunned, but instantly threw a ball of blue witchfire at me. I swerved and it only glanced off my arm, causing a stinging, tingly feeling like an electric shock. Then she turned and took off through the woods, moving surprisingly quickly. But I was taller, faster, and more ruthless. As I gained on her, she threw another spell at me, but she simply wasn't strong enough to stop me. Within seconds I had tackled her, pinned her to the ground with my knee on her chest, and had her wrists bound in the *braigh*. There had been times when just achieving this much against a dark witch had been a life-or-death battle. Catching Patrice had been comparatively easy.

Patrice's face was rigid with fear and astonishment, her dark blue eyes wild, the irises surrounded by white. With interest I noted that the *braigh* wasn't actually burning her wrists—a good sign. The more corrupt your soul is, the more the spelled *braigh* hurts.

"Seeker?" she whispered, trying to suck in breath.

"Not exactly," I answered, pulling her to a standing position with me. She collapsed instantly, falling against me, and I brought her up sharply, wary of tricks. But she was bent double with sobs, holding her linked wrists in front of her face.

"Oh, Goddess, I'm so sorry! Take me to Robin. Is she all right? Make sure Robin's okay!" Huge, gulping sobs shook her body, and I had to help her back to the clearing.

When we got there, Patrice stumbled toward Robin. She sank to her knees and held her bound wrists out to me. "Just undo this for a minute while I take the binding spell off Robin. Please!"

I narrowed my eyes at her, thinking. Then I knelt and said

the spell that opened the lock on the *braigh*. The silver chain dropped into my hand, and Patrice instantly took one of Robin's hands and gasped out a spell I recognized. Robin blinked and moaned, starting to shift. Patrice reached out to help her, then realized how incongruous and unwelcome that would be. She drew back and like a child crawled toward me and held out her hands. I put the *braigh* back on her, and she sank down on her side, giving over to racking wails that filled the air with remorse.

I knelt by Robin and saw that she was coming around. I spoke to her softly, explaining what was happening and checking her pupils, her pulse, her breathing. She seemed more or less her usual self, though she was upset and trying not to weep. She looked past me at Patrice, and her face contorted with shared pain. Then, unbelievably, she rose and went over to Patrice and patted her shoulder. Patrice was ashamed and put her fists in front of her face, hiding her face in the ground.

It was a while before Patrice's grief subsided enough so that she was relatively coherent. I sat about ten feet away, leaning against a tree, not interfering. If I were a Seeker, I would be doing all sorts of things. But now I had the freedom to let things be, at least for a while.

Eventually Patrice blinked and looked around at Robin.

"Oh, Robin!" she said, fresh tears flowing. "Oh, I'm so sorry! Are you okay? Are you okay?"

"I'm okay," Robin said.

"There's no excuse for what I've done," Patrice said. She lay on her side, curled up in a ball, staring straight ahead. "I deserve to have my powers stripped." She squeezed her eyes tightly shut against that new pain.

"What is all this about?" Robin asked more firmly than I'd heard her speak before.

"It's Joshua," Patrice said, trying not to cry. "He's not getting better. I feel like we're losing the battle. I've tried everything I can think of, but I'm just not strong enough. I couldn't think of what to do. Then one night after a circle I felt so energized, so powerful. I went home and transferred some of my power to him. It all went on from there." She shook her head in disgust at her actions. "I've betrayed you, the coven—everything I believe in and have worked for. I betrayed Joshua—how could I have done this to him? Made him a party to my crimes? Oh, Goddess!" Once more she began crying, until it seemed there would be nothing left inside her.

"Is Joshua better after you transfer power to him?" Robin asked.

"Yes, for a bit. But it doesn't last long. He's losing weight again, he's covered with an awful rash that makes him miserable, he's all puffed up from the steroids—I don't know what to do. I've always been able to solve problems, but I can't solve this." Patrice sniffled and rubbed one wrist against her nose, then looked up at me. "How did you know?"

"Your friends were concerned about you," I said. "I followed you tonight, after the circle."

Patrice nodded, ashamed. "Things were going on, getting worse and worse. I hated myself, but I couldn't stop. The only thing that mattered was that I somehow make Joshua better. But thank the Goddess you stopped me before I went any further."

Robin seemed subdued but not at all angry or withdrawn—more tired.

"You've saved me from myself, you've saved yourself and the rest of the coven from me, you've saved Joshua from having a complete monster for a mother." Patrice seemed exhausted and resigned and full of remorse. But relieved. It was over. "I don't know what will happen to me now."

Slowly she got up, with her and Robin supporting each other. Robin seemed a bit more wobbly, and I offered her my arm.

"You should go home," Robin told Patrice. Without Celia here, Robin seemed to be taking a more active role. She seemed less flighty somehow, stronger, more authoritative. "Can you take the *braigh* off her, please?"

I hesitated. "Is that a good idea?"

The two women stared at me in astonishment.

"What do you mean?" asked Robin.

I shrugged uncomfortably. "Patrice seems to regret what she's done. I believe she's truly sorry. But what she was doing—or was about to do—wasn't shoplifting sweets. What would have happened if I hadn't followed you? Would I be looking for your body?"

"That spell wouldn't have killed Robin!" Patrice said, horrified.

"It probably would have," I said with quiet assurance. "It probably would have killed any witch who wasn't very strong. And Robin's energy had already been sapped—by you. At the very least you weren't doing her any good, were you?"

Patrice stared at Robin, mouth agape, as if realizing anew her colossal error. The idea that this spell might have actually taken Robin's life stunned her, and she wobbled on her feet, looking dazed.

"What are you proposing?" Robin asked, keeping an arm around Patrice to support her.

"I don't know, exactly," I said. "If I were a Seeker, I would turn her in to the council, and she would most likely have her powers stripped. As it is, I'm reluctant to do that. But I'm also reluctant to let Patrice go her merry way."

"We all need time to think," said Robin. "Let's just go home and think, and then we can try to decide what's best."

"What if Patrice runs off?" I didn't want to be hostile, but these two weren't facing the hard realities of the situation.

She looked at me, startled. "I can't leave. Joshua isn't strong enough to be moved—and I could never leave him."

My instincts told me she was telling the truth. I took off the silver *braigh*, and though she rubbed her wrists, her skin wasn't seared or red. "Are you all right to drive?"

She nodded, pale and wide-eyed.

"Right, then. I'll take Robin home. Everyone stay put and take it easy until we arrange to meet again."

Then the three of us picked our way back through the night-dark woods until we hit the trail again. We were each quiet and thoughtful as we got to the parking lot. Patrice climbed into her car, and Robin and I got in mine. And so ended Patrice's reign of power.

13

Morgan

When I got home from Practical Magick Thursday afternoon, I found Aunt Eileen and Paula in the living room.

"Hi!" I said, giving them hugs. "I feel like I haven't seen you in ages."

"Morgan, is that you?" Mom called, pushing through the kitchen's swinging door into the dining room. "Will you set the table?"

Wanting to visit more with my favorite aunt and her girlfriend, I glanced hopefully at Mary K. across the room.

"No way, José," she said firmly. "I already made the salad and pulled all the stringy things off the corn. I've been here since *four*."

Okay, she had a point. I got up and went to the kitchen to get silverware. A witch's work is never done.

"So I thought the family room was completely finished," said Paula as we were sitting down. "We'd been working on it after work every day for a week. It looked so great. I folded up the last drop cloth—"

"Must you tell this story?" Aunt Eileen said plaintively, but I could tell they were just teasing each other.

"Washed the brushes, hammered on the paint can lid," Paula went on, pulling her chair in next to mine. "We stand back, we look, the whole room is a soft, buttery yellow—"

"It was perfectly fine the way it was," Eileen put in.

"But when I went to hook the cable thing back up, I saw that the whole wall behind the entertainment cupboard hadn't been touched!"

"Lots of people wouldn't bother painting behind a huge, heavy piece of furniture," Eileen defended herself.

"The whole *wall*," Paula said, taking an ear of corn and passing the rest to me.

"I couldn't move that thing by myself," said Eileen, but we were all laughing at this point, and she looked sheepish. Paula winked at her across the table, and they both smiled like honeymooners.

"Why does this story not surprise me?" Mom asked, giving her younger sister a look. We all laughed more—it was fun to see adults still acting like real sisters. Mary K., on my other side, pointed her fork at me, like this was the kind of thing I would do. I gave her a big, fake smile.

"I was wondering if you'd heard from the agency," Mom said. "I remember you contacted them last week."

Aunt Eileen and Paula had been thinking about adopting a child.

Eileen nodded. "They sent us a huge packet of information."

"It was terrifying," Paula said. She speared a piece of chicken on her plate and ate it.

"We still just don't know, is what it comes down to," said

my aunt. "The idea of adopting a child in need is really compelling—a friend of mine at work recently adopted a baby girl from China. And one of our neighbors brought back a baby from Romania."

"But each of us had always assumed we'd have a baby of our own someday," Paula said. "There are just so many things to think about, issues to consider. Everything we think about seems to carry so much weight."

"We just have to keep gathering information," Eileen added. "I think the more we learn, the clearer our decision will become."

"Have one of each," said Mary K., talking through a mouthful of chicken. We all turned to look at her. She swallowed and nodded, her shiny russet hair swinging gently around her shoulders. "One of you has a baby, and then you also adopt a baby. Tons of people have two children. Isn't the average in America like 2.1 or something?"

Paula and Eileen stared at my sister as if she were a talking dog.

"We never thought of that," said Eileen, and Mary K. shrugged.

"Two children. It just never occurred to me," said Paula in bemusement. "I've been so wrapped up in trying to figure out how to have one."

"She has a point," said my mom. "If you started having your own baby now and put in the adoption papers, then two or three years from now, when the adoption comes through, they'll be the right age apart."

Just like Mary K and me.

"I've been offered a scholarship to study in Scotland this

summer." As soon as the words were spilling out of my mouth, my brain was already screaming for a shutdown. What had possessed me to blurt this out now? Five heads swiveled to look at me, five pairs of eyes opened in surprise. Morgan, shut *up*, I told myself, aeons too late.

"What?" Mom asked. "You haven't mentioned this. What scholarship?"

"I just heard about it today," I said, threatening myself with all kinds of revenge for being so stupid. "I didn't even know it existed," I added truthfully.

"What is this scholarship?" my dad asked. "Why is it in Scotland? How did you find out about it? Is it for math?"

"Um, Eoife McNabb called me today," I mumbled. I started pushing my peas around on my plate with my fork. "I don't know if you ever met her. But she's a . . . teacher. And she got me a full scholarship to go to a really exclusive, impossible-to-get-into college. I'm the only American they've ever accepted."

"Congratulations, Morgan!" said Aunt Eileen. "That's marvelous! This is really impressive!"

"Goodness, Morgan," said my mother. "I don't think I've heard you mention Eva McNabb. Is she one of the teachers at school?"

"Not exactly," I said, looking at my plate. "Um, the course is for eight weeks. I have to pay my airfare, but everything else is taken care of. It's a huge honor."

"Is this through the math department?" Dad asked again.

"Not exactly," I repeated in a small voice. There were several moments of silence.

"What is this a scholarship for, Morgan?" asked my mom in a calm, don't-give-me-any-crap voice.

Witchcraft? Magick? "Um, healing? Herbal medicine?" I said.

"You have a scholarship to go to Scotland to study *herbs?*" Mary K. asked in disbelief.

I looked down at my plate. "It's a famous place of learning," I tossed out into the deafening silence at the table. "Only the most learned and powerful . . . teachers are there. I'm the youngest person they've ever considered, and the only American. It's considered a huge honor—the chance of a lifetime. Tons of people would be ecstatic to be offered this opportunity."

I saw Eileen and Paula glance at each other—gee, they wished they'd stayed home tonight. Mary K. was looking fixedly at her plate. I could tell she wasn't thrilled about this idea. I didn't even want to look at Mom or Dad.

"It would be an education just to go to Europe," I said, starting to use my desperation tactics, none of which I'd thought through yet because I'd been *certain* I was going to *wait* until the right moment to bring this *up*. "I'd be in northern Scotland—surrounded by tons of history. Historical monuments. And then England and Ireland are just train rides away. Just visiting those would practically count for a world history credit. Think of the cities—Edinburgh, London, Dublin. Castles, gardens, moats." Okay, I was really stretching here. "And I would be working, working, working, not getting into trouble or being bored, or—"

When I finally glanced up, I saw my mom and dad looking at each other. I felt a familiar pang of guilt—I was their fish out of water, the egg some cowbird had left in their nest. When they had adopted me, seventeen years ago, nothing could have prepared them for this last year, as I was suddenly revealed as something they distrusted and feared: a witch by blood.

There was no way they would let me go, to further my study of Wicca, pushing myself one step closer to being an educated, accomplished witch. They were probably still fruitlessly hoping that something would happen to me and that I would somehow turn back into a Rowlands—go to MIT for math, get a nice engineering job or maybe teach. Get married. Have nonwitch grandchildren. Look back on my witch period the way they looked back on their flower-child years.

It wasn't going to happen.

"We need to discuss it," my mom said, her lips somewhat tight. I almost fell out of my chair. What? It wasn't an outright no!

"Yes," Dad said, swallowing. "There's a lot to think about. We need much more information before we can even make a decision. Is there some kind of brochure or something for this place?"

I was so stunned, I felt like I'd just been hit on the head with a golf ball. "Uh, I don't know," I stammered. "I can ask Eoife. She can give you more information."

Mary K.'s large brown eyes were opened wide.

"I'll do anything you say," I put in, trying not to sound pathetic and desperate.

"Well, your grades have been acceptable lately," Mom said, not looking happy. She stabbed her fork into her salad, and I felt I could have heard the crunching from three blocks away.

"There haven't been any recent . . . incidents," my dad said, his mouth in a tight line.

I looked down. There was a lot they didn't know about. But it hadn't been my fault. Most of it. When I looked back up,

Aunt Eileen and Paula were gazing at me solemnly. It occurred to me that I had no idea what they thought about my involvement with Wicca. I was sure Mom had told Eileen about some of it at least. They were really close, despite the difference in their ages and the different paths their lives had taken.

"We realize that you feel that . . . Wicca is somehow important to you," Mom said. "While it's true we're not very happy about it, we also know that not everyone can live the same life."

"If you let me do this, I will never ask for anything again," I swore.

Mom looked at me for the first time, a smile quirking her mouth. "You said that when you wanted Rollerblades. And now look at you. Still asking for things."

That broke the tension a little bit. Mom and Dad looked at each other again.

"At any rate, we'll discuss it," said Dad, pouring himself another glass of wine. "We're not promising anything. We're only agreeing to think about it."

"Thank so much," I breathed. "That means so much to me."

"Excuse me," said Mary K. "Who's going to give me rides to the beach this summer?" Her eyebrows raised as she looked at me pointedly.

"Um, Alisa's dad?" I suggested. "The church youth group?"

"Whatever," Mary K. said with a big sigh, but I felt it was her way of letting me know this somehow wouldn't kill her.

I looked back down at my plate, suddenly starving. This was amazing. If I didn't know better, I'd swear I had put a spell on my whole family.

"Oh, my goodness," Mom said, looking up with surprise. "We never said grace tonight."

"No, you're right," Dad agreed, thinking back.

"Let say it now," I suggested. I felt an overwhelming gratitude in my life right now and wanted a chance to acknowledge it. I felt that any thanks given to any god all went to the same place, anyway, no matter what religion you were centered in.

We all held hands and bowed our heads. It was a tiny bit like a weekly circle, and I felt comfortable and relaxed. My mind was still whirling with the possibility that my parents might actually consider letting me go to Scotland.

Dad began, "Oh, heavenly father, we your children who are bowed before thee thank thee humbly for the gift of this our food tonight. Your mercy is never ending, your constancy eternal. . . ."

As Dad said the familiar words, a feeling of peace and happiness came over me. I was surrounded by my family, Scotland wasn't out of the question, and I felt safe and as far away from Cal Blaire as I could possibly be.

Dad finished, and we all said, "Amen." And my heart was full of gratitude.

Right after dinner I talked to Bree, who agreed to say that I was sleeping over at her house. She wanted to help with my nightmares, and since my parents knew that Bree and I wouldn't get wild or anything, it was okay with them.

Around eight I said good night to Aunt Eileen, Paula, and the rest of my family, packed a bag, and drove to Red Kill. Alyce's apartment over Practical Magick was like Alyce herself: comforting and appealing. She opened the door at once as soon as she sensed me on the stairs.

"Come in," she said. "Hunter isn't here, and Bethany stepped out for a minute. But come in and sit down."

I sank into her chintz sofa, and Whistle, one of her cats, jumped up on my lap, smelling Dagda. By unspoken agreement we talked about light things—the weather, our gardens—I had dug mine just recently and was starting to fill it in with herbs and flowers. It wasn't long before we felt Bethany on the stairs, and then the three of us sat and waited almost half an hour for Hunter. In the meantime I told Alyce and Bethany about my offer to go to Dùbhlan Cuan. They were really pleased for me and seemed impressed. They both really hoped I could go and offered to talk to my parents if I'd like.

Hunter finally showed up, looking stressed and a little preoccupied. He came over and gave me a quick kiss, then noticed my questioning expression. "I'll tell you about it later," he whispered, and brushed his fingers along my cheek. Then the four of us settled down with cups of herb tea—no caffeine—to go over the strategy.

"Will this thing be able to find me here?" I asked, thinking that if it couldn't, I could just move in.

Bethany nodded. "We believe so. It's your consciousness that it traces, or at least that's the theory. Tonight we're going to work on the assumption that as it's getting more insistent, it will simply need to take on a somewhat less amorphous form. But even if it's barely present, we're prepared to handle it."

I thought of Cal as he'd been when I'd met him, glowing and charismatic, a teenage Wiccan god. How had it all come to this?

Alyce showed us the chunk of brown jasper she had gotten. It was the size of a softball, and though it was shot through with interior flaws and occlusions, it was still beautiful and impressive.

"You'll be sleeping in my bed," Alyce said. "The three of us will be magickally cloaked. Your role will be to go to sleep and be as powerful as you can. Did you bring your mother's tools?"

I nodded and kicked my backpack gently.

"You'll surround yourself with protection spells that will limit anyone who attempts to bind your powers. Then you'll go to sleep and wait for Cal to come to you. Once he does, once he makes a connection with you, you will need to, in your dream, actually take hold of him. Hold him and don't let go. Our theory is that what happens in your dream will be mirrored in real life."

"So you'll just wait while this thing approaches me while I'm asleep?" My voice sounded tight with tension.

"We'll absolutely be on the alert and able to get to you in a moment," Bethany assured me. "There will be three of us, joining our powers. Once you have a hold on the thing, we'll trap it with the binding spell we created. Then we'll further encase it in the brown jasper. And I think that should be the end of it."

"And you're quite sure Morgan won't be hurt?" Hunter asked.

"We'll be right here," Alyce said. "She certainly couldn't go anywhere."

"Does this sound all right with you?" Hunter asked me. "If you're afraid, we don't have to do this. We'll think of something else." He rubbed his hand across his eyes, and I noticed the dark circles there.

"No, it sounds okay," I said. "It's frightening, but not as bad as the idea of having more dreams like this. I just have to stop them."

"Okay," said Alyce, standing up briskly and gathering our cups. "Sounds like we've got a plan, then."

I went into Alyce's bathroom and put on my mother's magickal robe. It was a deep green silk, embroidered with symbols, runes, and letters. As usual, it felt comfortable and light against my skin. When I wore it, I was never too hot or too cold—it was always perfect.

I went into Alyce's bedroom, which I'd never seen before. Once again it seemed to embody its occupant. The bed looked overstuffed and comfortable, the colors were shades of lavender and green, and there were fresh flowers, a crocheted runner across the dresser, and the scent of soothing rosemary and chamomile. Alyce, Bethany, and Hunter were performing cloaking spells on themselves.

At the head of the bed I placed one of Belwicket's silver cups, with water in it. I also placed my birth mother's wand there. Around the other three sides I placed the other three cups, to represent earth, fire, and air. I got into bed, sinking into the comforting softness, the fresh, clean-smelling linens. I had the Belwicket athame, the one engraved with generations of initials of Riordan witches. Someday, I would have my own initials engraved on it, too.

I pulled up the covers and tucked the athame at my side. Surrounded by the powerful tools that had helped women in my family work magick for hundreds of years, I felt fortified and more confident. I felt connected to the long line of witches who were my ancestors and a special connection to

Maeve, the woman who had given me up for adoption rather than allow me to be killed by Ciaran MacEwan.

Hunter came over and tucked me in. "Got your spells ready?" he asked. I nodded. "Right, then—sweet dreams. When you see me next, all this will be over." He leaned over and kissed me, then went back to Alyce and Bethany, who were opening the window and removing its screen.

Alyce came over, smiled, and patted my shoulder. "This will all be okay," she said.

"All ready?" Bethany asked. I nodded. "Good luck, then."

Alyce turned off the light. I looked at the luminous hands on my watch—it was ten-thirty. I often stayed up later than that, but at the moment I felt completely wiped. Closing my eyes, I took in a deep breath, trying to relax and concentrate. *Just relax,* I told myself. *Relax. Everything is all right. You're safe.*

"Of course you're safe," Cal says, sitting on the edge of the bed. I jump—I hadn't sensed him coming.

"Why are you doing this?" I ask. "What do you want?"

He leans over. "I want you, Morgan," he says. "I always did. You never would join with me the way I wanted. But now you will." He smiles and strokes my hair, and I can't help flinching. He doesn't seem to notice. "Tonight you'll be mine, all mine. You didn't take any of those nasty potions that kept us apart." He frowns at that. I try to think of what I'm supposed to do now. I can't remember.

Then Cal cheers up. "But tonight is different," he says, smiling again. "Tonight I'm here, and he's not. Tonight you and I will join completely."

"I don't want to." My voice comes out sounding faint, and I say it again, more strongly. "I don't want you. I want you to leave me alone."

Cal tips back his head and laughs, exposing the smooth brown skin of his neck. "Of course you don't really want to be alone," he says, sounding indulgent in a way that pisses me off. "Not when you can be with me. Didn't you have too many years of being alone? You did. But now you'll never be alone again."

"What are you talking about?"

He takes my hand, and it really feels like a person holding it. His skin is smooth and warm, and I feel the brush of the leather friendship bracelet he used to wear. When he was alive. I shiver, but again he doesn't seem to notice.

"You've been playing hard to get," he says. "I don't blame you. You're an exceptional witch—very strong. You're simply too strong not to be joined with me." His smile lights his face, and I'm struck by his physical beauty. "You know what they say—if you're not with us, you're against us."

"Who's us?" I ask. I know I'm supposed to do something, something guided or interactive—but what? Desperately I try to remember—I'm supposed to do something, for some reason. . . .

Cal shrugs casually. "With me. Tonight you're going to join with me forever."

"No."

He laughs easily. "You don't really have a choice, Morgan. Not anymore. Not tonight."

"I always have a choice." My voice comes out stronger than I intended, and it makes his golden eyes flick over at me.

"Not really. Not against me." He stands up and holds out his hand. "Now, come on. Let's get going. I've waited too long for this. You won't get away from me tonight." He remembers to smile at the last bit, but it's a horrible, almost vicious expression, and I recoil.

"No," I say, pulling farther back into the bed. What should I

do? What should I do? Isn't something supposed to happen now? Is someone supposed to help me? Where are they?

Cal reaches forward and grips my wrist in a tight, almost painful grasp. My eyes narrow a bit—I'm not a pushover. Not anymore. I'm no longer innocent Morgan, never had a boyfriend, so flattered that a demigod like Cal Blaire would want me. He thinks I'm weak, is counting on it. But I'm not weak. I'm very strong, and I know it. I'm so strong, I can protect myself in this situation. Strong enough to fight Cal all by myself. I can win. I can beat him.

"Why are you doing this? I want you to leave me alone," I say firmly. I tug on my hand, but he doesn't release it. "I don't want to be with you. I'm not going to join with you. You need to leave and never come back."

He frowns. "Morgan. Stop it. This is nonsense. Now, come on." He gives a hard yank on my hand and almost pulls me out of the bed. My shoulder feels a sharp pang, as if my arm is straining against its socket. Determinedly I pull it back.

I realize now that we're in the meadow again. I don't remember where we were just seconds ago. But we're in the meadow, and there's Cal's bed at the edge of it. The sun is warm on my hair, the bees' droning noise is mesmerizing—it's the most perfect, peaceful place in the world. Except Cal's in it.

Time to act. I reach forward and grab Cal's other hand, pulling it toward me. He smiles—playful Morgan—but I keep a death grip on it and won't let go. He frowns in puzzlement and tries to pull his own hand back. "Let go," he says.

I send every bit of power I have into the hold I have on his hand. "No," I say calmly. "I won't let go."

He suddenly gives a hard yank, and I hold on tighter, clenching my teeth. "You can't hurt me anymore," I grind out—

Then my eyes opened to darkness lit only by a glow of blue witchfire. I lurched up in bed and stifled a horrified scream—in my hand I was holding one leg of a dark-feathered hawk! The same hawk I had seen in all my dreams—the one with the cold, golden eyes. My face froze in shock as I took in the scene—the hawk's huge, powerful wings beating the air, my fist gripped around its leg tight enough to break its bone. The hawk screamed unbearably loudly, right in my face, and I squeezed my eyes shut, the horrible sound raking my eardrums.

Its beak lunged toward my face, and I ducked at the last second to avoid having my cheek ripped open. Around me I heard a commotion—moving and shouting, and then a light flashed on. Other hands were grabbing at me—I was on my knees on the bed, hanging on to the hawk's leg, avoiding its beak. Then I recognized Alyce's voice, and Hunter's and Bethany's, and it was enough to pull me back into reality. Hunter managed to grab a beating wing. Alyce grabbed the other one, holding it hard, outstretched against her body. A sudden slash made me cry out, and I saw that the hawk had managed to slice into my arm with its other taloned claw.

I let out a gasp, and then Hunter grabbed the other leg, and between the four of us we held the hawk down. It struggled fiercely, still lunging with its beak, and then Alyce reached out one hand and grabbed its neck. Her face was contorted with fierce, ruthless determination—I had never seen her look like this before.

I still held on to one leg and glanced down at the gashes on my arm, dripping blood. I stared at the hawk, at its golden eyes—they were like Cal's eyes. I looked up at Alyce to ask what should we do now, but I saw a look of horror come over her face. My head snapped back to the hawk, and then my jaw dropped in terror as the hawk's mouth opened and a wisp of thick, oily smoke emerged. In a second I remembered the last time I had seen something like that—it had been back when Selene had died, in her library. It was here now, and it was incredibly foul, this close. Just being within proximity of it made me feel like my life force was draining away, as if it was the coldness of death itself. My heart sank and my mouth went dry, and then, as the last of the smoke roiled out of the bird's mouth, it went limp and sank lifeless in our hands. It was dead.

"Quick!" Bethany shouted, dropping the bird's body on the bed and throwing herself toward the window. She slammed it down and locked it, and Alyce sprang for the door and locked that, too. I was still trying to get my bearings, but the other three witches were circling the anam, grim looks of resolve on their faces.

Then, as we watched, the nebulous smoke slowly began to achieve more form. It coiled upon itself, becoming more three-dimensional. My eyes felt like they were burning as a grisly, acid-eaten face gradually emerged from the oily fog.

It was Selene.

My mind went blank with terror. Selene! My first thought was that against Cal, we had good odds of beating him. Against Selene, who besides Ciaran was the strongest, most evil witch I'd ever come across—our odds were much worse.

Selene! How was it possible? Her anam must have been within the smoke that drifted from her mouth when she died. She must have found some other host—this hawk, or another one, or something else. Then she had decided to take revenge on me. It hadn't been Cal at all. It had never been Cal.

I felt my heart sink at this realization. The real Cal was dead—he had been dead all this time. Selene had used his image in my dreams to make me follow him. She must have known that I still had conflicting feelings about her son: anger, fear, maybe even a little fondness. But most of all, guilt. He had sacrificed his life for me. And as much as I knew he was a twisted person who had done terrible things, a small part of me still regretted that. Because he might have truly loved me, in his way. And because he never really had a chance. Not with a mother like Selene.

Her death's-head grin was becoming more apparent—in life, Selene had been as beautiful as Cal, in the same sleek, golden, feline way. She was no longer beautiful. It was as if every bit of evil she had in her had eaten away at her human form, leaving only the grimacing mockery of a challenge.

Without thinking I threw out my hand, and a jagged, neon blue bolt of energy snapped from my fingers and sliced right through the smoky form. Her slash of a mouth widened in horrible amusement.

I was stiff and stupid with fear. We hadn't prepared for this. I felt pearls of cold sweat popping fully formed on my forehead, felt the ache of adrenaline tightening my muscles, the dull pain of my stomach, tight with terror. Selene.

Alyce made an incoherent sound—she and the others had been muttering spells nonstop since the hawk had died—but now I looked down and saw that dark tendrils were spinning off from lower down, and they were beginning to curl around the legs of Hunter, Alyce, and Bethany. They each quickly tried to jump away but already seemed held. They were throwing witchfire at it, spitting spells at it, and nothing they were doing was having any effect. These three witches were all strong, quick, and knew well how to protect themselves—but not even Hunter seemed to be able to stall her attack.

The smoky tendrils were weaving themselves higher, coiling insidiously around their bodies.

"Why are you doing this?" I shouted. I was going to sit here and watch my friends—and my *mùirn beatha dàn*—die, and then I was going to die myself if I didn't figure something out. A horrible, risky idea was starting to take form in my mind. I rejected it, but it kept coming back, and now I saw it as perhaps my only hope. It would be dangerous, and I didn't know if I could pull it off. I didn't even want to try.

"If it's me you want, take me, and leave them alone!" I cried.

The horrible Selene face laughed, and I realized that she wanted to see them die, that she would enjoy it. I found my mother's athame in my hand, glowing with a white heat, and without a plan I leaped forward and plunged the blade into the middle of the smoke. To my surprise, Selene actually seemed to feel it—the smoke recoiled and the face gasped. Then her expression twisted with anger, and a dreadful, perforated voice emanated from it. "You can't stop me, Morgan," it said, every word feeling like a steel nail scraped down a blackboard. "You're not strong enough. I'll take my revenge. My kind have been waiting hundreds of years to wipe out your kind, and I'm not going to let my own death stop me. You're the last of Belwicket, the last of the

Riordans. Once you're dead, true Woodbanes can continue their work. I'm willing to martyr myself to that cause. Soon we'll be more powerful than you could possibly imagine."

Twining vines of smoke slid toward me, running up the bedspread like fire. I edged back against the wall, then looked up to see that Bethany's neck was entwined—she was choking and gagging, and her face was tinged with blue. Bethany was going to die. Alyce and Hunter had turned their energies to saving her, but Selene's march toward death seemed unstoppable.

Unless.

Fully formed, my mother's power chant, the power chant of Belwicket, came to me, as it had on so many other occasions. The ancient, beautiful, and sometimes harsh words spilled from my mouth as I kept my eyes locked on Selene's form. *"An di allaigh an di aigh an di allaigh an di ne ullah. . . ."* I kept the words flowing like lifesaving water as my hand crept across the bed to the body of the dead hawk. My half brother Killian had caught a hawk once by calling its true name. If you know the true name of something, you have ultimate control over it. I knew Ciaran's true name, but no one knew mine, including me. My fingers brushed the soft feathers, felt the absence of a life force, and I included the hawk's true name in my chant.

Selene was hardly paying attention to me—perhaps she thought it would be amusing to see what I could come up with, what puff of breath I could throw against her turbulent hurricane of power. Bethany was almost unconscious now, and the coils were moving up Alyce and Hunter. I saw hard intent in his face but no fear, and my heart felt a searing pain at the thought of what he was going through and how he was facing it.

I remembered what it felt like to be wolf-Morgan. My

birth father, Ciaran, had taught me a shape-shifting spell. I didn't remember most of it, but now I called on ancient Riordan power, the power of my mother and her mother before her, back through the generations. *Help!* I sent the message silently. *Mother, help me. Help me now.*

I closed my eyes, swaying for a moment as new words, at once unknown and familiar, streamed into my mind. I recognized the form of limitations of the shape-shifting spell, and silently I repeated them, putting everything I knew, everything I felt, every need I had into the words.

I was frightened, deathly frightened, yet felt I was pulled inexorably toward this future, this one direction. Silently I murmured the true name of the hawk. Then the pieces came together in my mind in a beautiful, dazzling, stained-glass window of magick, the three things I needed weaving themselves together in a spell so balanced and perfect and beautiful, I wanted to cry.

Bethany sagged in Selene's grasp. Alyce and Hunter were now fighting the deadly tethers around their necks. There was no more time—not one second.

"Rac bis hàn!" I shouted, throwing my arms wide. Selene whipped around to look at me. *"Nal nac hagàgh! Ben dàn!"* I had a moment to see her gaping, protruding eyes widen in shock, then I was forced double, and I was screaming in pain.

Even Alyce and Hunter stopped struggling to watch me, and I cried out, instantly regretting my decision through a thousand hours of ripping, racking pain that lasted less than a minute. My bones bent unnaturally, my skin was pricked with thousands of needles, my face was drawn forward like burning steel. There was no way of getting through this with dignity or even a show of bravery. I wailed, screamed, cried, begged for mercy, and finally ended up sputtering incoherently, lying on my side on the bed. I blinked and struggled to rise. The room was strange and hard to understand. My feet couldn't clutch the bed well, and I gave a clumsy hop so I could perch on the footboard. Hesitantly I flapped my wings, felt the latent power contained within.

I was a hawk. I had shape-shifted. I now had a hawk's laser sight, razorlike talons, and merciless, ripping beak. I sent a message to Selene: Catch me if you can. Then I gathered my wings to me, and with a brilliant burst of immense joy and an aching longing for air and freedom, I took flight, right through the closed and locked window. I felt the wood splinter, the glass shatter against my chest, but then I was soaring up, up, into openness. I heard glass raining down, and then, with a soft sound, my wings caught fire and I streaked through the sky.

A few, exhilarating moments later I sensed another hawk coming after me. It was Selene, back in the body she had usurped. However, that body had already been dead for several minutes, its systems breaking down, and as I glanced back for a millisecond, I saw that it flew with jerky, uncontrolled movements, working hard to keep up with me.

Yet right now Selene seemed unimportant. A hawk's wild joy ignited in me as I wheeled effortlessly through the dark night air. I felt incredibly light and incredibly strong. A thousand scents came to me as I soared higher—the higher I went, the thinner and cooler the air was as it filled my lungs. I heard the flames on my wings whip fiercely through the air, but I felt no pain, no heat, only a terrible, righteous anger and an increasingly strong need for revenge. As ecstatic as I was, shooting through the night, my thoughts once again turned toward Selene. She had been haunting me all this time, appearing to me in Cal's form. She wanted me dead. She wouldn't ever stop until I was dead and the dark Woodbanes were able to flourish. I couldn't let that happen.

I tucked one wing slightly in and began a huge, sweeping arc at sixty miles an hour. The dark hawk was slowly gaining on me, and even from this great distance I saw the glint of hatred in it golden eyes, the overriding lust for my death, and I knew that this could end in only one way: her death. My victory.

Once more I began saying the Riordan power chant, hearing the words unspool in my mind, feeling my power strengthen and swell.

I'm a Riordan, I thought. I'm the *sgiùrs dàn*. This will end here, and my descendants will go on to help Woodbanes be everything they can be, on the side of good.

Then, like children responding to a dare, we squared off and faced each other, hovering for a moment in the onyx-colored sky. I felt everything in me coil and hesitate, and then, like a bolt of witchfire, I hurtled through the night toward Selene, aware that she also was streaking toward me. I was both falling and soaring, my wings tucked close, feet drawn up: I was a weapon, going eighty miles an hour downward toward my enemy.

I was on Selene so fast that I didn't have time to really expect it—it was only a few seconds before we were swerving at the last second so we wouldn't just crash into each other. Quickly I circled as tightly as I could, and then I let all my raptor instincts take over—I quit thinking like a human, quit being Morgan altogether. I let go of all that and let my hawk free.

I don't know who drew blood first—Selene or me. But we attacked at the same moment, and my hard beak shot forward and seized her flesh, pulling and ripping. I tasted her blood, warm and salty, at the same instant I was aware of a searing pain in my right shoulder. The next several minutes were a blur of feathers and fire and a fine mist of blood arcing through the air. Selene's feathers were scorched by my fire, and the acrid smell of burned feathers filled my sensitive nostrils. Harsh, raucous screams filled the air, upsetting and distracting me—and then I realized I was making them. Finally with one huge surge of power I rose up just enough to be able to clamp one of my vicelike feet around Selene's thick neck. It reached around and I squeezed my grip as tightly as I could, as if Selene were a rabbit and I was about to have lunch.

In a frenzy Selene's dark wings beat the air around me, obscuring my sight. But still I hung on. It was impossible to fly and hold on at the same time, so I swung my wings when I could and concentrated on closing, closing, closing on Selene's neck.

This is for Cal, whom you destroyed with your evil, I thought grimly. This is for me, whom you haunted and terrorized. This is for all the people you've hurt or used or killed. You are going to die here and now, at my hand.

When I had been a wolf, I had been seized with an overwhelming lust for the hunt, a palpable desire to track prey down and rip into it. I had been able to stop myself at the last second when I realized my prey was Hunter. I felt no such inclination to stop now. Every tenet I had been raised with against murder, against revenge—disappeared now as I felt myself slowly pressing the life from Selene's body.

We were spinning now, falling toward earth in a death spiral. I was unable to keep myself aloft and hold on to Selene at the same time, so I allowed myself to fall. Selene was still beating her wings, but more and more weakly. My claws, holding her neck, ached with the pressure, the tension of staying tight, but I was locked onto her and there was no way I would let go. I glanced down and saw with a sickening realization that the ground was rushing up to meet us. Soon I would crash, probably breaking every bone in my body. I didn't think even a hawk could survive that kind of collision. But at least I would take Selene with me.

All at once I felt the life force of Selene's hawk blink out. One breath later I was sure of it—the hawk was dead. I was maybe fifteen feet from the ground, and I loosed my talons and let Selene drop heavily to the ground. Then I began beating my wings backward furiously—how to land? I didn't know!

I did the best I could, slowing myself as much as possible and setting my feet in front of me. I ended up crashing, anyway, my feet running against the ground, my wings outstretched, but I lost my balance and tumbled head over claw several times in what must have been the most humiliating hawk landing ever.

Still, I didn't break anything, and as soon I stopped rolling, I was up on my feet and leaping over to Selene. Just as I got there, the hawk's mouth opened, and once again the oily black smoke began to coil outward. I slammed my foot around its neck, crushing it shut, holding it ruthlessly.

It was horrible—the dead bird's battered and bloody body

flopping and struggling against me. My own blood running into my eyes and stinging them. The oily smoke of Selene's anam stopped short. This close to her, I felt her panic, her intense fury, her hatred, her venom and malice. I flapped my wings to keep my balance, hopping awkwardly on one foot while the other held on. It seemed like hours later, but at last I sensed the final, twitching, muffled death of Selene's anam. Trapped inside a dead being with no escape, she could not survive.

Selene Belltower was no more. Yet I didn't let go, not for a long time, not until the shaking of my muscles forced me to release my grip.

Then I released my hold, folded in my wings, and began the agonizing process of becoming myself.

Selene was dead, and I had killed her.

And I wasn't sorry.

14

Hunter

We got Morgan cleaned and patched up at Alyce's. She felt terrible about the broken window, and Alyce looked at her like she was insane when she offered to pay for it. Bethany didn't think any of her wounds actually needed stitches, but she did put butterfly bandages and poultices everywhere. Then I brought Morgan to Bree's house, about half an hour before the sun came up. We woke her up, and she helped me put Morgan to bed. I said we'd explain later. As soon as I was sure Morgan was asleep and safe, I took off and went home.

Once there I took a long, hot shower, getting blood and pain and evil off me. I dropped into my bed and passed out cold.

"Here, lad, have a cuppa," Da said. I heard his voice and groaned, but then the tantalizing scent of strong tea reached my nostrils and I struggled to surface.

I propped myself up on my elbows and took the hot mug. "Cheers."

"How are you? You look all worn out."

I moaned. "Don't ask. I've had better weeks. What time is it?"

"Oneish. I've been thinking about that witch, Patrice," Da went on.

"Me too," I said, and told him about everything that had happened with Patrice and Robin in the woods last night. I sighed. "I'm thinking that maybe I should ask her to turn herself in to the council. I hate the idea, but I don't know what else to do. Despite how sincere she is, now that she's done something like this, I just can't see never keeping an eye on her again. And next time she would be much more subtle, more experienced. I don't know."

I took a big gulp of tea. Ahhh. "I know that if she absolutely refuses to turn herself in, I won't make her," I went on. "I won't strip her of her powers against her will. That's a bloody awful business."

"Well, maybe you won't have to," Da said. "Look." He took out a black-and-white composition notebook. "I've been working on a translation, from Middle Gaelic. It's been very unusual, very enlightening. It seems to have been a textbook from a Wiccan center of learning, back in the 1500s. I've been finding some incredibly unusual spells, and they're almost all to do with limiting powers in some way."

"Really?"

"Yes. I mean, these spells haven't seen light of day, as far as I can tell, in hundreds of years. When I was studying for my initiation, I never even touched on this category." He flipped past pages covered with his fine, scrawly handwriting and began reading me pieces of his translation.

My brain wasn't quite up to par after the events of the last two days, nowhere near enough sleep, the trauma of having

Morgan go through what she had. I squinted up at my father.

"I'm not getting it," I said bluntly.

"Look," he said, a deliberately patient tone entering his voice. "I'm saying we take the basic form of this spell here because it does things in stages and can be broken up. Now, this spell"—he flipped through several pages—"is interesting because of how it sets out its limitations at the beginning, and the best thing is that it doesn't seem to be tied to the phase of the moon. This spell has a really good ending in how it wraps things up, seals things, in the way it controls its effects. So see? We take these parts from these three spells—plus one or two phrases from a couple of others—and create one spell from them. What do you think?"

I struggled to make sense of it. I sat up and took the notebook from him, flipping back and forth between the marked pages, reading his careful translations and margin notes. Slowly the picture began to seep into my troubled brain. My jaw dropped at its implication.

I looked up at Da. "Oh, Goddess—do you think it could work?"

He sat back on his heels, pleased. "I think it might."

"You are absolutely bloody brilliant," I said, and he laughed, tilting back his head.

"Can I get that in writing?" he said.

We took a couple of hours to carefully write out the whole, new, complete spell. The two of us went over it again and again, checking and cross-checking everything. Around four, an uncharacteristically domestic Sky brought us some tea and sandwiches, as well as some sample oatcakes from a recipe she was trying out for Beltane.

"They're great," I said, practically spitting crumbs. "Go with it."

At last we felt ready.

Da and I were very familiar with the spell; there seemed to be no loopholes in it—it was exciting, different, as if we were about to make Wiccan history. Da must have felt this way about the dark wave spell, having created something beautiful and terrible out of nothing. It was funny, when I'd first found him in Canada, he'd been a mess. Now he really seemed to be excelling. It made me proud to be his son.

We drove over to Thornton, to Patrice's house. We'd called ahead, and she was expecting us. When we got there, she was alone, which surprised me. I would have thought she would have called, if not Celia or Robin, then at least some other friend or colleague.

"Thanks for meeting with us," I said as we stood awkwardly in her foyer. She looked tired and somehow beaten, as if she was going to give up now, since her most desperate plan hadn't worked.

I introduced her to my father, and like Celia and Robin, Patrice was a bit impressed to meet the dark wave destroyer. I let Da explain what we wanted to do.

"From what I understand, you've worked magick that could almost certainly get you stripped of your powers," Da said in his forthright way.

Patrice flushed and hung her head, the edges of fear showing in her eyes. "I know," she said, barely audibly.

"However, no one in authority knows about it yet," I said. "But anyone who knows about this will never forget it. Because there's always the possibility that you'll drift back to dark magick."

Her face blanched at these stark words.

"So you seem a bit dangerous, do you see?" I asked, not meanly. "Once someone crosses the line, it seems so much easier for them to cross it again. People will be watching you, waiting for it to happen. But my father has crafted a spell that seems to address this particular situation. We believe that we can work a spell around you that will satisfy others' fears about you."

"You want to strip my powers," Patrice said dully, looking at the floor.

"No. We want to limit them, forever. But in a very specific way," Da explained.

"It's a bubble spell," I said. "A spell that affects your powers in a certain way for the rest of your life. As of today, it can't be undone. Your powers wouldn't actually be limited in strength, but in effect: if you agree to undergo this, you'll never again be able to affect any other living thing with your magick again."

Patrice gave me a quizzical look.

"You'll be able to make magick, beautiful, powerful magick. You'll be able to celebrate and take part in magickal rites. You'll be able to affect stone, mineral, air, and earth as much as you can now. But you won't be able to affect your son's health. You won't be able to rid yourself of the smallest headache. You won't be able to create a sleeping draught for a friend. You won't be able to do the peas-times-three spell on your garden."

She gave a slight smile at the mention of a very basic spell that every witch child learns.

"You won't be able to call your dog with magick; you won't be able to scry to see other humans or animals or plants. But you'll be able to learn, to teach others, to witness magick, to participate, to feel the joy and satisfaction of creating something beautiful from nothing—just like any other witch."

"But because I can't affect any living thing, I can't harm anyone with dark magick," she said, looking thoughtful. "And neither could I help anyone with good magick."

"That's correct," Da said.

"I hate this," she said calmly.

"It's the best option you have right now," I said.

"You're right," she said, years of strain and fatigue in her voice. "How long will it take? I have to give Joshua his medicine at eight."

"It will take about forty-five minutes," said Da.

Trying not to cry, Patrice led us to her small circle room, in what used to be a butler's pantry, off her dining room. "Let's do it, then," she said.

It took longer than forty-five minutes because neither Da nor I had ever done it before. We also hadn't had an idea of what effect it would have on Patrice physically, and at one point she became so nauseated, we had to stop for a few minutes. But we followed each step carefully, as we had written it, and by a few minutes after six we said the final ending words.

When it was over, I felt drained and hungry. Da dismantled the circle, and I edged away and sat with my back against the wall. Patrice simply lay down on the wooden floor, right where she was, looking white and ill. Da also seemed very tired, but it was he who went to the kitchen and came back with a pitcher of iced tea and a package of cookies.

"I raided your fridge," he said cheerfully. Slowly we ate and drank, and afterward we all felt better. I fetched a wet washcloth for Patrice's forehead, and she seemed glad to have it.

"Do I look different?" she joked weakly, and I shook my head.

"No. I don't even know if you'll feel different or how the spell will take effect," I said. "You were the guinea pig. But if it works, it could save a great many witches from having their powers stripped in the future."

"Then it will be worth it," Patrice said. "Now I need to go tend to my son."

I went to Morgan's house after that. Mrs. Rowlands let me in, smiling pleasantly, even though I knew she wasn't thrilled with the idea of Morgan dating a witch.

"Hello, Mrs. Rowlands," I said. "I was wondering if I could see Morgan."

"I'll call her down," Mrs. Rowlands said. "You aren't going to believe what she looks like. Apparently she and Bree were trampolining in Bree's backyard this morning, and Morgan managed to bounce off and crash right through a lilac hedge. She's a mess." Tsking and shaking her head, she went to the stairs, where Morgan was already on her way down, having sensed me come in.

I looked at her solemnly. She did look like a wreck, but there was a relief in her eyes, a lack of fear, of tension, that hadn't been there in ages. For that I was glad.

"I told you that trampoline should have a safety net around it," I said.

"Hunter Niall: Wiccan smart-ass," Morgan said in disgust a few minutes later. "That will be the title of your biography."

We were out on the double glider that had recently made its spring appearance on the Rowlandses' front porch. We had some iced jasmine tea, and Morgan had also managed to supply some zucchini bread.

I gave her a little smile and put my arm across the back of the glider, resting against her shoulders. We would have to go over the events of yesterday in depth, but not tonight. "Good story, by the way." I paused. "When I was in the house, I felt Alisa upstairs."

Morgan nodded. "They're going to the nine o'clock movie downtown. Dad's taking them. I think Alisa might be sleeping over."

"Good." I hesitated before I brought up the next subject. It was an idea I'd had a couple of days before, but it had seemed impossible then. It might not be impossible now. "How strong are you feeling?" I asked.

Morgan looked up at me with curiosity and shrugged. "You mean, after yesterday?" I nodded. "Actually, though physically I feel like crap, magickally I feel pretty strong. It's like every time I go through something that should have killed me, when I come through, I just feel stronger."

I smiled. "There's something I'd like to ask you to do for me," I said. "Not tonight. But tomorrow. It involves your magick."

15

Morgan

"How's my little acrobat?" Hunter asked, kissing me and hugging me to him as we walked to his car.

"Ouch. Don't squeeze too hard."

We got into his car, and he looked at me as he started the engine. "Are your parents thinking of suing Mr. Warren?" he asked seriously, and I whacked him on the leg, remembering too late that virtually every part of my body was sore. "Ow!" I laughed, cradling my hand.

He and I hadn't talked much about what had happened with Selene and my shape-shifting. It was as if we were both too freaked out about it and needed time to process it individually before we delved into it together. For right now I wanted to pretend it had never happened.

We headed out of town. It was a beautiful Sunday. My parents, Mary K., and Alisa had gone to visit a garden. I'd wanted to go, but Hunter was more important. Dagda and I had slept in, and I was actually feeling a tiny bit better. "So what are we doing?" I asked, watching the late April sun sparkle on the new green leaves of the trees.

"I wanted you to meet Patrice, the witch I've been working with in Thornton," Hunter said. "And her son."

I gave him a questioning look. He had given me only the vaguest information about the case he was working on with his father. He'd told me the day before that they'd reached some kind of resolution, which I guess made it okay to tell me her name and where she lived, but he didn't seem inclined to say more than that, like why he wanted her to meet me and why she would want to see him again. I just tried to relax and enjoyed the ride. I had never been to Thornton but saw that it was cute and old-fashioned looking in kind of the same way Red Kill is. Hunter drove through the town and into a residential section. He stopped in front of a large, beautiful Victorian home.

"Whoa," I said. "I love this house."

The door opened as we approached the porch. I hadn't really formed much of a mental picture of Patrice Pearson, but she was more normal looking than I had imagined. She didn't look all that witchy, and she didn't look one bit evil. She smiled, seeming a little shy or embarrassed, so I tried to act like I knew nothing of what had been going on. I picked up weird vibes from her, though, as if part of her aura was under a sheet.

"Hello, Morgan," she murmured, holding out a strong, dry hand. "I feel like I've heard your name mentioned before."

"Hi," I said, shaking her hand and still wondering what I was doing here.

"Hunter said you'd like to meet my son," Patrice said,

increasing my curiosity. "He's down this way." She gestured down a hall that led toward the back of the house. I looked behind me and shot Hunter a what's-going-on look, but he only raised his eyebrows at me.

We went through a large, homey kitchen that looked fresh and pristine but like it hadn't been updated in sixty years. Old-fashioned sink, antique stove. Patrice opened a small door off the kitchen, and I stopped in my tracks.

My senses picked up on illness and pain, fatigue and hopelessness. Hunter had mentioned Patrice had a son but hadn't said any more than that.

I followed Patrice into the room, Hunter behind me. The room was small and looked like it might have been a sunroom at one time. Cheerful posters hung on the walls, and the bed linens were printed with race cars in primary colors. There was a large TV and a DVD player and a stack of videos nearby. But everything else about the room screamed hospital—the hospital bed, the IV stand next to the table, the cabinet covered with more medicines than I could count. And of course, the little boy, thin and listless, with a tube running under his sheet. He didn't even look up when we entered the room. The TV was turned to some kind of nature show featuring alligators and getting right up close to them. His eyes watched the picture, but they were dull, lifeless. He wasn't really seeing anything. His body looked emaciated beneath the sheet, but his face was round and swollen looking.

Patrice seemed unbearably tense in here and with good reason. "Joshua, this is Hunter Niall and Morgan Rowlands," she said, unnaturally cheerfully. "Morgan wanted to meet you. She heard how brave you've been." She looked at me, and I saw that she wasn't entirely sure why I was here, either. But now I was beginning to understand. I smiled at Joshua and then turned to Hunter.

His gaze was measured, questioning.

I hesitated, then gave a tiny shrug and nodded.

"Oh, Patrice," he said now, turning to her. "Would you mind showing me that book on New York gardening I saw in your living room?"

They left me alone in the room with Joshua.

Now he looked at me with suspicion. "Are you a doctor?"

"No, no," I assured him. "I go to high school. I thought I'd just hang out for a while, that's all. So, you've got a lot of equipment here. What's this thing for?" I touched the IV stand. Over the next ten minutes Joshua and I talked about his leukemia, his graft-versus-host disease, how his mom took care of him, and how tired he was. It was all I could do not to just hang my head and burst into tears. But I didn't.

Instead, as Joshua talked, I very gently put my hand on his arm, picking up on his vibrations, his aura, his life essence. I felt his bony little shoulder through the sheet, and it reminded me of my own injured shoulder, which still throbbed painfully. I gently traced the side of his head, grinned and tapped his chin, and then pretended to tickle the bottoms of his feet. He gave a halfhearted grin.

I sat down in my chair again. "Joshua, is it okay if I just put my hands here for a few minutes?" I asked, putting one hand on his upper leg and one on his chest. He nodded warily.

"Gosh, what is that crazy guy doing with that alligator?" I said, and he turned his gaze back to the TV.

I closed my eyes and relaxed everything, letting go of my

tension, my distaste for the smells of disinfectant and illness, the scent of plastic and medicine and clean sheets. The faint noise of the TV faded. I sank into a midlevel meditation, where I consciously dissolved any barriers I felt between the outside world and me. After several minutes I felt that I was one with everything in the universe and it was one with me. There were no beginnings, no endings, only a calm, joyful communion among all things. And between Joshua and me. I let myself sink into him, into his tortured and weakened body. I let myself flow over him and inside him and through him. I felt his pain, artificially dulled by strong drugs; I felt his system being weakened yet also helped by other powerful and toxic medicines. I saw the normal white blood cells in his bloodstream but also cells swollen with fluid, about to burst; I saw Joshua's body being attacked from inside by his new marrow's immune system. His feelings became mine, and I swallowed down the nausea, the pain, the feelings of despair and hopelessness, the guilt he felt for upsetting his mother, the anger he felt, but didn't show, that this was happening to him.

I saw and felt it all, as if it was a Chinese puzzle knot, made up of countless ribbons twisted and knotted together in an incomprehensible way. I let myself sink deeper. The battle with Selene, and the resulting physical and emotional toll it had taken on me, had left me not at full power. But I thought I had enough to do something.

I felt like a universal solvent, able to go anywhere, see everything, unravel anything. One by one I teased out ribbons and followed them. I traced them back to his bone marrow. I traced ribbons back to each of his drugs. There was a ribbon for pain, a ribbon for anger, a ribbon for his original leukemia.

I have no idea how long I sat there. I was dimly aware of my hands growing warm, but Joshua didn't seem to notice or care. I thought at one point Hunter came back to check on me, but I didn't look up, and he didn't say anything. A tiny bit at a time I unraveled the puzzle knot. I eased his new marrow into working harmoniously with his body. I eased his body into a joyful balance within itself. I soothed blood vessels, irritated tissue, muscles taut with pain. I brought Joshua more into balance with the Goddess, with nature, with life. As things became more normal, more recognizable, I felt a general lightening, as if Joshua and I were free, soaring in the air, nothing weighing us down, no cares. As usual it was beautiful, mesmerizing, and everything in me wanted to stay in that magickal place forever.

But of course I couldn't.

When at last I raised my head and blinked, I saw that Joshua was deeply asleep in front of me. I shook my head as if trying to wake up and looked around to see Hunter and Patrice both sitting on chairs, watching me with solemn eyes. I looked back at Joshua. He looked different. His skin tone seemed more natural to me, his eyes less sunken. His sleep was restful and calm, his face unlined and free of pain. I quickly cast my senses and picked up on a balance, for lack of a better word. He felt more balanced.

I, however, felt like I was made out of Silly Putty. I didn't know if I could stand.

"Uh," I said, looking at Hunter. He immediately came over to help me stand up. My legs felt wobbly, rubbery. I felt hungry and tired. Patrice was watching me with a mix of emotions on her face. I straightened up with difficulty, then forced back my shoulders and took a deep breath. I gave Patrice what I hoped was a reassuring smile.

She looked from me to Joshua, then stepped past me to her son. She took one of his hands and held it against her cheek. He moved a little in his sleep, but to me it seemed like his puffy face was looking more normal, his limbs less stiff, his movements freer. I smiled at him.

Hunter put his arm around my waist, and I looked up to see a world of love and trust and awe in his green eyes.

Patrice turned back to me, looking grateful and scared and amazed all at the same time. She could tell he was better—anyone could. I didn't know how much I had done, but I knew I had helped somehow, to some degree.

"Who are you?" she breathed.

I thought of who I was, of everything that had gone into making me what I was, the long line of witches and women who had lent me their strength—it was mine to use, in this lifetime.

I smiled at her. "I'm Morgan," I said. "Daughter of Maeve of Belwicket."

"Morgan, you look incredibly beautiful," Hunter said for the fifth time.

I looked up at him, flushed with pleasure. This was pretty much the most effort I had ever made with my appearance, and by all accounts it was paying off. I was wearing a clingy top of a soft sage green. It had a deeply scooped square neck and three-quarter sleeves. I wore a silver chain with a piece of amber on it around my neck.

The skirt I had ordered from a costume shop. It was

made of layers of tulle, different shades of green, a layer of maroon, a layer of pink—seven layers in all, all sewn to a tight-fitting waistband. The bad thing about being built like a boy was that I usually looked like a boy. The good thing, if there was one, was that my waist actually looked small and kind of girlie if I wore a big, poufy skirt like this.

On my feet I had dark green ballet slippers, real ballet slippers, which were like wearing nothing. I had bought white ones and dyed them three times.

I had given Mary K. free rein with my makeup, and I had to admit that she had a promising future as a makeup artist. My eyes had never looked so big or luminous, my mouth looked lush and feminine, and my skin looked dewy and fresh. Not only that, but I had actually submitted to having my long hair turned into soft, fat ringlets that hung past my shoulders. I had been afraid of looking like Little Orphan Annie, but instead my hair just looked kind of wild and natural and sexy.

This was one of the very few times in my life when I felt actually feminine and strong and beautiful. And the effect it had on Hunter had cheered me up to no end. His eyes had been on me ever since he picked me up. Now he was looking deeply into my eyes over the top of his sparkling cider, and I was feeling incredibly attractive and womanly, as if I had bewitched him. It was a great feeling.

"Morgan! Fabulous!" said Bethany, sweeping past. I called hi after her, but she was already whirling away.

"How many people are here?" I asked, edging closer to a table.

Hunter glanced around. "Close to eighty, I would guess. I think all of us ended up asking everybody we knew."

It was twilight on Beltane Eve, and we were in the same

woods close to the spot where Hunter and I had had our picnics with Bree and Robbie. Tonight it looked enchanted —tiny glass lanterns with votive lights were everywhere, and there were tables covered with all sorts of food and drink. Sky and Raven, the organizing committee, had outdone themselves. Garlands of fresh flowers swooped from tree to tree. A tall, beautiful maypole stood in the center of the clearing, and it was hung with long, silken ribbons in rainbow colors. Sky had recruited musicians from various covens, and the haunting, lilting strains of magickal Irish music were weaving their own spell over everyone.

"Where did Sky get the maypole?" I asked.

Hunter grinned, moving closer to put his arm around my waist. "It's a mast, from a boat shop. She and Raven picked it up and had to transport it here, sticking out of Raven's back window."

I laughed, picturing it. My eyes automatically sought out Sky, and, sure enough, she and Raven were together by a food table, their heads bent together, talking earnestly. Hunter and I glanced at each other. They did care about each other, I knew. I hoped their relationship would work itself out.

"They did a great job," I said. I picked up some slices of fruit, admiring the platters of oatcakes, bowls of honey, herbed tea with flowers floating in it, cakes decorated with edible flowers—pansies, Johnny-jump-ups, marigolds, nasturtiums.

"Sister! Hello!" I smiled and groaned at the same time, turning to see Killian coming toward me, a glass of wine in his hand. As usual he looked cheerful and irreverent, his longish hair streaked with shades of auburn and caramel.

"Hi, Killian," I said, and Hunter greeted him, too, as civilly as he could manage.

"Niall," Killian said, then turned back to me. "Super party! Great eats, music—you went all out. What hand did you play in this?"

"I showed up."

"Sky and Raven organized everything," Hunter said evenly, and I made an effort not to grin.

"Ah." Killian gave a quick glance around, and of course, there were Sky and Raven, about twenty feet away, shooting looks at him that, if they didn't kill him, might certainly maim him. But it took more than that to upset my half brother. He smiled at them hugely, raised his wineglass in a toast, and then prudently headed in another direction.

"Ciao!" he called back to me, and I waved.

"Maypole! Maypole!" someone cried, and the musicians came closer. Sky organized volunteers, male-female, male-female, and handed them each a ribbon. Then, as the music started, the dancers began to move in opposite circles, weaving in and under, over and under each other, and as we watched, the colorful ribbons were woven around the maypole in an even pattern of diamonds. It was beautiful, and I was glad we were continuing this old tradition.

Without speaking, Hunter and I linked hands, keeping one hand each free so we could eat and drink. When night fell, a huge bonfire was lit, and Hunter took me around, introducing me to people I didn't know. Everyone seemed to have a distinct reaction on hearing my name. I was about to ask Hunter about it, but then he pointed out where the star cluster Pleiades would rise, right before dawn the next day. At Samhain, six months from now, Pleiades would rise right at sunset. Beltane and Samhain marked the two halves of the year.

Hunter and I wandered away from the light and noise and music, talking about everything, huge, tiny, sad, funny. I had seen Patrice earlier for just a minute, and she had told me that Joshua no longer needed a feeding tube. His doctors were mystified, but he seemed to be shedding his illnesses like a snake's skin. She held my hand tightly and thanked me several times with an intensity that brought tears to my eyes.

"So Da and I are off to England in a month," Hunter said. We were far enough away so that we didn't need to speak loudly anymore.

I sighed.

"Your folks still haven't made up their minds about Scotland?" he asked.

I shook my head. "They've spoken to Eoife, but they really don't understand why there aren't any brochures for them to look at or a Web site."

Hunter laced my fingers with both his hands. "I want you to go," he said seriously.

"I feel I need to," I agreed. "They haven't shot it down—at least not yet. They want to see my end-of-year grades, et cetera. I've actually been carrying good-luck stones in my pockets. The thing is, if you're in England and I'm here, I just don't know if I can bear how far away you'll be. If I'm in Scotland, you won't be so far away, and I won't feel so panicky."

"I know what you mean," he said. "I hate the thought of being separated from you, by any kind of distance or time. But I know I have to go home for a while to see people. Da is doing a bunch of workshops about the dark wave spell, and I'm going to join him for some lectures about this new bubble spell."

"I'm so proud of you," I said, squeezing his hand.

He grinned. "It feels good to do something of real use. To possibly prevent witches from having their powers stripped—witches who have just made bad decisions or are about to. And this could effectively lessen the council's power. Which might pave the way for a new council or an adjunct council."

We stopped then and looked around, realizing we had been walking and talking, so caught up in each other that we had gone farther than we'd meant to. I couldn't hear the music or laughter at all anymore, couldn't see the light from the bonfire.

We were in a tiny clearing, no more than ten feet across, with a perfect overhead view of the indigo night sky and stars. Around the edges of the clearing was an unusual ring of violets—the last violets of the season. It looked magickal, like fairies had created this place. And we had ended up here. It felt like fate, not coincidence, that we were here.

Then I looked at Hunter, and he looked at me. My heart fluttered, and Hunter led me to the center of the violet ring. He sank down on the fine moss and pulled me down next to him. The delicate, sweet scent of the violets perfumed the air around us as we lay side by side, and when I looked up, I felt like I could see all of the sky before me, as if I were flying.

"Morgan."

I looked in his face. He looked unusually solemn, the dancing light in his eyes strangely absent. Slowly he traced one finger down my arm, and I watched as his touch left a tiny trail of sparkling shimmer wherever it touched. Smaller and finer than sparks, lacking heat and leaving only the very faintest tingle, the shimmer continued down my side and onto my skirt, wherever he touched.

I held him to me and touched his face, his angular, carved cheekbones. To me right now in the moonlight, he seemed heartbreakingly beautiful—strong and masculine, familiar and intimately trusted. He had seen me at my absolute worst and still loved me. He had seen me sick, angry, making mistakes, being stupid—and he still loved me. He had been patient and kind, demanding and true. I loved him with all my heart and believed that he absolutely loved me—not because he said so, but because he showed me he did, every single day.

I took his hand and pressed it to my chest. I could feel him shiver a little, which made me smile. I loved the fact that this calm, cool ex-Seeker—a witch who was in control in virtually every situation—consistently lost control when it came to me. Then I coiled my hand around his neck and pulled his face closer to mine. He seemed hesitant, waiting, and to dispel any doubt I opened my mouth and kissed his, hard. I suddenly felt like I had opened a dam and was now being swept away by torrents of water much stronger than I was.

We moved together, our mouths locked, our arms and legs clinging to each other as tightly as they could. Hunter paused and kissed me gently, then pulled back and looked in my eyes, lifting his hand and making a slight motion toward the sky. Immediately I saw movement above, and then we were covered in a soft wave of flowers, flowers raining from the sky—roses, peonies, daisies, too many to count. I laughed. This was the joy of Beltane—this pure love of nature, of life, of love itself.

I looked into the deep green of Hunter's eyes, moved by the intensity of the love I saw there and stunned by the intensity of the love I felt for him. Was it possible for one person to care this much about another? I felt like I couldn't get close enough to him.

Hunter kissed me again, and legs and hands got tangled in my skirt. We were gasping in the cool night air, rolling together so that first he was on top and then I was. I loved having him under me, being able to hold his face in my hands, to feel like what happened was up to me. Which it was.

There, on Beltane Eve, celebration of fertility, life, and love, Hunter and I made our own celebration, our own timeless commitment to each other, our wordless promise to be true to our love, to protect each other, to revere and respect each other always, as long as we lived.

Epilogue

"You are going to miss me so much," Hunter said confidently. Another scratchy announcement said the flight to Cleveland was now boarding.

Morgan laughed. "You think so, huh?" She put her arms around his waist, aware that the flight to London was going to start boarding any minute.

"I know so," he said. Then he lowered his voice and pushed her hair off her neck. "And I know I'm going to miss you, so much."

"It won't be for that long," Morgan reminded him, feeling the telltale prickle of tears at the edges of her eyes. Do not cry, she told herself. Do not waste time crying.

"It will feel like a long time," he said. A man dragging a suitcase big enough to hold a dead bear pushed past them on his way to Gate 17. Hunter moved them a bit to the side. "I have something for you." He pulled a small box out of his pocket, and her eyes flared. Speechless, she opened it. Inside was a silver claddagh ring, two hands holding a heart between them and a crown on top of the heart. On the heart was the rune Beorc, for new beginnings.

"It's beautiful," Morgan breathed, her fingers clumsily trying to get it out of the box. He helped her slip it on.

"I'm so proud of you, Morgan," he said softly. "I'm just incredibly proud. And incredibly happy. And incredibly in love."

Her eyes definitely felt watery now, but she swallowed hard. "I know exactly how you feel."

She threw herself at him one last time, the silver ring a comforting weight on her right hand. They hugged and kissed until they heard the boarding call for the flight to London. Then she let go of him and went over to her family. Her parents looked mildly uncomfortable at the public display of affection, but now they smiled and hugged her hard. Morgan's mom had tears in her eyes, and so did Mary K.

"I'll be back before you know it," she said. "And Mary K., feel free to borrow any of my clothes while I'm gone."

Mary K. rolled her eyes. "Like that will get me anything," she said. Laughing, Morgan hugged her tight.

Morgan stepped back next to Hunter, who touched her cheek gently, as if for the last time. "We'll see each other soon, you know," she said as she slipped into his arms.

Suddenly the noise of the airport ceased to exist and time stopped moving altogether. "I love you, Morgan," Hunter said, and the words surrounded them both in a warm and colorful flow of magick. For one final moment they were alone, together, in a world that held no one else. Then time began to move forward again, and the people around them regained their voices and resumed their movements. "I wanted a perfect moment with you," he said, his green eyes sparkling with magick or tears—she couldn't tell which.

"You'd better get going, sweetie," her mother said, and gave her a final hug. Morgan picked up Dagda's carrier, made sure she had her tickets and carry-on, and headed down the gate to the waiting plane. She turned back one last time and waved.

The future was opening up for her like the petals of a flower. She would be the strong witch she had always wanted to be.